The Closing of the Day

Friendship in the Shadow of Goodbye

Eric V. Litsky

Contents

Dedication

To my incredible wife, Norma.

You are the calm in my chaos, the spark in my inspiration and the heart of all I create.

I am endlessly grateful to walk this journey with you.

With all my love, always.

Prologue

Present Day

The sound of footsteps crunching in yesterday's snowfall was all that could be heard as Tommy, his wife Julie, and Mia, their five-year-old daughter, walked silently through Burnside Cemetery.

The barren branches of the oversized oak tree filled the space above her gravestone as if protecting it with outstretched limbs. Tommy hadn't been there since they laid her to rest some twenty years earlier.

The tree was full of late summer leaves back then. The heat of the day, softened by the first whispers of autumn. The air was filled with the scent of fresh cut lawn. And the heavily fragranced floral arrangements brought over from the funeral home to accompany Mia's simple pine casket had long since withered away.

She died as she had lived, alone. Suddenly, Tommy was abruptly brought back to the present by the sound of his daughter's whining.

"Are we there yet, Daddy?" asked Mia. "You promised we'd go to McDonald's if I behaved. I've been good. Haven't I?"

Julie slowed their pace down, allowing for Mia's small strides to keep up. "In a minute, sweetie. Daddy wants to visit an old friend," she added.

"It's right over here," Tommy said. He stopped at the highly polished granite stone which marked her grave.

MIA CHILDS
1964-2002

He placed a long stem red rose on the grave. How can a life be summed up with nothing more than a name and a few dates?

She never made it to her 40th, he thought. She never married or had children. Probably never even had a lover. She died before she ever really lived. She lived a small life in a dying town.

Tommy couldn't remember the last time he cried. There were so few times in his life he actually let the tears roll down his face. He cried the day his daughter was born. And when he and Julie graduated together from the University of Connecticut.

And he cried the day he punched his father square in the face and walked out of the only home he had ever known. That was also the day that Mia Childs died.

"Mommy, Daddy's crying," said Mia, frightened at the thought of her father in pain. Julie put her arms around him, pulling him close as he wept. Years of pent-up emotions opened up as the salty tears streamed down his face.

"It's OK, sweetheart. She knew how much you cared," said Julie.

"Daddy is OK, honey. He's just sad remembering his friend. He needs to cry and will feel all better soon," she added, bringing little Mia into their family hug.

Little Mia reached up and took Tommy's hand.

Chapter One

Spring 2002

East Hartford was a tired old blue-collar town. Its political leadership lacked the foresight and energy to move forward into the new millennium. Some would say the town was just too stubborn to die. Like Camden to Philadelphia and Troy to Albany, East Hartford suffered from a *second city syndrome*. It was an *also ran* - the horse that finishes last. An almost. A might have been. But never quite was. Hartford got the state capital, insurance and banking. East Hartford got the manufacturing, the three-decker tenements and the drugs, crime and corruption.

Pratt & Whitney Aircraft, known to the locals simply as *The Aircraft,* employed a fraction of the workforce it had in its heyday during the Vietnam War. The skilled workers have steadily moved on to greener pastures, along with the state-of-the-art manufacturing plants which have sprouted up all over the sunbelt. But not in East Hartford.

Main Street, once fully occupied with locally owned shops, now showed vacancies on every block. Shoppers took their dollars to the Buckland Mall in the neighboring town of Manchester. A million square feet of national chain stores a few miles away is too much competition for Main Street. What was left was a sorry assemblage of karate studios, nail salons, luncheonettes, and laundromats. And the sure killer of every community – adult bookstores and bars.

Vehicles traveling along Main Street revealed an eclectic mix of pick-up trucks and older cars with rust spots. Many were cheap foreign models. From time to time you could see a highly polished Mercedes with dark, tinted windows slowly passing, its stereo booming out the pulsating beat of the bass, to accompany unintelligible hip hop lyrics. Everyone knows that's the drug dealer's car. Only a fool or a junkie would get near that car.

The downtown movie theater had been closed since the 12-plex opened near the highway a decade earlier. It's now a nightclub. Thursday is heavy metal night. Friday is Latino night. Saturday is hip hop night.

Sunday is visiting day at the hospital, a place where bad choices land many of it's clientele in the ER.

The white boys hang out behind the Walgreens on Main Street. There was a thick cement wall that runs behind a dozen parking lots for an entire block in the rear of the Main Street stores, creating a two-foot elevation change from the street. An urban skateboarder's dream.

Most skateboarders could jump it with ease. The good ones could do a full 360°. It was East Hartford's version of the X Games. The lot was a haven for teenagers, full of graffiti and broken glass. A broken basketball rim without a net hung precariously off its backboard. It was an easy place to vacate in a hurry if you were being chased. You could exit to three streets by car, two alleys by bike or skateboard, or run through half a dozen backyards by hopping short fences.

Tommy Green spent his early teen years there learning the complexities of life. It was there where he made friends, smoked his first cigarettes and touched his first breast. It was where he learned how to fight. And how to run. Depending on the size of his opponent.

Tommy tagged his initials *TAG* with a can of red or black spray paint on whatever clean surface he could find – as if to say, "I am here. See me." He was always large for his age. Most people pegged him as older than his 17 years. He was shaving every other day by the time he was 15. Now, two years later, his beard with three days growth was heavy enough for him to do the weekend beer runs without getting carded. If he stopped shaving on Wednesday, he looked 21 by Friday. At six feet three inches, he was half a head taller and twenty pounds heavier than each of his friends.

The football coach at East Hartford High School wanted his size and strength on the offensive line. But Tommy wasn't much of a jock. He especially didn't like getting yelled at by coaches. He did try the wrestling team once, in the 189 lb. weight division. These were very powerful young men. His first and only match was against the more affluent suburban Glastonbury High School. It ended in his school's disqualification.

Actually, it was more like a riot. That's how the East Hartford Journal reported it the next day. Tommy was getting tossed around the mat by a much more experienced Glastonbury wrestler. He got frustrated and punched the Glastonbury boy in the mouth, splitting his lower lip open and knocking out his two front teeth. Blood splattered everywhere as all hell broke loose. It took the two referees, a dozen parents, and several teachers and staff to separate the student wrestlers who went after each other with such fury.

In the ensuing melee, the principal broke his glasses and had his wallet lifted. His Visa card and $60 somehow ended up in Tommy's gym shorts. In addition to the forfeit, Tommy was tossed off the team and suspended from school for two weeks.

From that day on, no one ever messed with Tommy Green. Had he known that a single punch would earn him a reputation of a real *bad ass* for the rest of his time in high school, he would have hit someone years earlier. The suspension felt more like a reward. He had some extra walking around money thanks to the principal. He could sleep until almost 10 a.m. each day, and still be on time at the condo project in Glastonbury where he worked.

He was a part timer on the maintenance crew there during the school year but picked up two weeks of full-time work now that he was out of school. He didn't have to put up with high school crap for two weeks. It was like a vacation. A paid vacation.

Tommy's mom died when he was six. That's when his dad started drinking heavily. When he drank, he got mean. And he drank almost every day since he got laid off a year earlier from *The Aircraft.*

Tommy stayed clear of him. His dad was an angry man with a bad temper.

Tommy's dad was called Mr. Green by everyone, including his son. Few people knew that Aldridge was his first name. A name that he always thought belonged on the leaderboard at a golf course rather than on the scoresheet at the bowling alley, where he felt more at home. Mr. Green rarely wore anything but jeans and a white crew neck tee-shirt. Usually a size too small for his increasingly widening body. He had a gut around his midsection from years of fatty food and alcohol.

Tommy often joked with his friends that he had six-pack abs while his dad carried around a quarter keg. Now in his 50's, Tommy's dad still had powerful arms. His left arm sported a US Marine Corps tattoo. The right one was a pirate's flag. Over the years it had faded. The skull and cross bones now looked more like a smiling light bulb. His favorite expression, *semper fi, motherfucker*, was always spoken at inappropriate times. He was a living, breathing caricature of what those in more polite circles refer to as *trailer trash*.

"When the fuck are you going to get a haircut and wash that orange shit outta your hair," Mr. Green barked in more of a statement than a question. "A couple of years in the Marines will straighten out your sorry ass."

"Mr. Green, will you get offa my case. I'll be 18 soon enough and outta here."

"What's all this shit about being suspended?"

"That pussy wrestler from Glastonbury called me white trash. So, I popped him in the face. I didn't mean for it to get that crazy. But he had it coming," protested Tommy.

"Next time, wait until you're outside. Then you can beat the crap out of that snotty bastard. And you won't catch so much shit. Fucking rich people think they got a right to piss on the rest of us. It ain't right. It ain't right at all," Mr. Green said as he flipped on the television and opened a beer can in one seamless motion.

Tommy knew any time Mr. Green got distracted was a good time to get away from him. He was dressed, out the door and on his way to work before the first commercial flickered on the 36-inch Panasonic TV.

Chapter Two

M ia Childs pulled her six-year-old Camry out of the Georgetown Village condominium complex, narrowly missing the rusted-out Chevy Nova driven by Tommy Green.

"Damn it!" she shouted, thinking how that crazy kid almost ran her off the road. She made a mental note to talk to the condo board about the maintenance people. They should be seen and not heard. Better still, not seen and not heard. She paid $325 per month for the HOA maintenance. That should entitle her to some peace, quiet, and safety, as well as a little courtesy.

The maintenance crew were teenagers. A half dozen really obnoxious kids. Her mind wandered a bit more about how they'd end up there. Was she judging? Probably. But she was in no mood to be gracious.

As she drove down tree-lined Hebron Ave. to her 10 a.m. doctor's appointment, she replayed in her head the message Dr. Barclay left on her answering machine last night.

"This is Dr. Barclay calling. I have the results of the CAT scan we did the other day. It is important that I see you as soon as possible. Tomorrow morning at 10 is open for me. I'll give you whatever time you need. Please call my office in the morning to confirm."

His not saying, "don't worry," or "it'll be alright," made her tremble with fear. She knew something was wrong. It had been months since the last time she felt really well.

She'd been too tired for too many months. She had mono as a teenager, but this was different. It was an achy tired. Each day another part of her body hurt. The blood tests revealed a concerningly low white blood cell count so, as a precaution, Dr. Barclay ordered a CAT scan.

Mia was 38 and, other than this bout with God knows what, she was in pretty good shape. She didn't smoke, and except for an occasional glass of white wine, she didn't drink. Some years ago she even stopped drinking coffee and developed a taste for green tea. She'd read that it had all sorts of healing powers.

She was careful about what she ate and made her twice weekly appearance at the Bally's Health Club.

Her blood pressure and cholesterol numbers were great according to Dr. Barclay. But she felt like crap and was beginning to get puffy around the eyes.

Mia lived alone. Always had. She'd have a blind date once in a while but that never seemed to develop into anything more than dinner and a movie.

She never knew her father. And her had mother moved to Tampa five years earlier after bitterly complaining about the Connecticut winters for most of her 74 years. She passed away last year.

Their relationship had been largely confined to a 10-minute call placed each Sunday evening just before *60 Minutes*, which neither of them wanted to miss. There wasn't much to talk about with her mom. A brief phone call was all that was needed to get the update on who died and from what, and who was getting married or divorced.

Now Mia was almost 40 and alone. No family. No siblings. No man in her life. No social life to speak of. Her friends were mostly just work associates. She could always count on the girls in the office to remember her birthday, and for her boss to remember *Administrative Professionals Day*. But not much beyond that. No one from the office had ever been to her home.

She was a legal assistant for a mid-sized Hartford law firm. Ten pompous lawyers all puffed up with their own self-importance, with twice that number of underpaid assistants doing the grunt work.

Coleman, Terrance and Paesano, PC was not the happy law firm its colorful marketing brochure described. A Republican Jew, an Irish Democrat and an Italian who despised politics, offered its clients a myriad of legal services with three distinctive personal styles.

Of the three partners she was happy that she worked for the Italian guy in the real estate finance department. At least he had a good sense of humor and treated her decently. The two other named partners didn't even know her name.

Her workday consisted of organizing files and double-checking figures for closings. When it was busy, there could be simultaneous closings in each of the three conference rooms.

Today would be quiet. Nothing was scheduled.

It was Friday and she called in requesting the last of her allowable sick days for the year. A year that was not nearly half over.

She drove her beat-up Camry to Dr. Barclay's appointment. She was alone and she was scared.

Dr. Barclay's office was located within a brown shingled, two-story, older medical office building. It was an architectural eyesore. An ugly building with a few neatly trimmed evergreens in front. She thought an array of bright colored flowers would be a welcoming touch which would maybe help soothe its patients' anxieties.

The building had a couple of dozen physicians' offices. It seemed to Mia that each office specialized in a different body part.

Dr. Barclay had a general practice and handled a wide variety of patient maladies. Though he was fairly stuffy and humorless, he had kind eyes and she felt he really cared about her health.

The waiting room was cheerful enough and the magazines were fairly current. The mood music which emanated from the hidden ceiling speakers was early Beatles performed by some unknown string quartet.

The music wasn't helping, and Mia needed to settle her nerves. She once took a yoga class. Although she hated stretching into those uncomfortable positions, she did learn to breathe more deeply from her diaphragm – to help calm herself when she was stressed. She found herself breathing more evenly and calmly when the receptionist called her.

"Mrs. Childs, the doctor will see you now. Second door on the right."

Mia hated it when it was assumed she was married. She wasn't a Mrs., was too old to be called Miss, and never got comfortable with Ms. Why couldn't they just call her Mia instead of needing to designate her marital status?

Mia's thoughts continued to jumble around. When she was scared her mind raced, often focusing on unimportant things like grocery lists or a plot twist in a television series she had been watching.

The second door on the right was not an exam room but Dr. Barclay's office. She took a seat in one of the two well-worn but still comfortable brown leather chairs in front of his highly polished mahogany desk.

She had been a patient of his for eight years but had never been inside his personal office. Her visits were limited to one of six exam rooms where Mia often found herself partially naked, fighting to get comfortable on the paper-covered exam table.

The exam room was always too cold and there was generally nothing to read but the patient information pamphlets, pointing out the merits of the particular drug the pharmaceutical reps were pushing.

It was mid-morning and her stomach churned from a combination of hunger and worry. All she had was a cup of tea and a non-fat yogurt when she awoke five hours earlier, startled from a nightmare she could no longer remember. Mia hadn't slept well in months.

She glanced around the small office, cluttered with family photos and trinkets from the doctors life. His neatly framed medical degree was from McGill University. Americans call McGill the Harvard of Canada. Canadians refer to Harvard as the McGill of the US. She never knew he was educated in Canada. *At least it wasn't one of those Caribbean medical schools*, she thought to herself.

Dr. Barclay opened the office door at precisely 10 a.m. She always thought it rude when doctors kept patients waiting. Her time was valuable too. Mia was thankful Dr. Barclay ran a tight office and rarely kept her waiting more than a couple of minutes.

He was a tall man, a little over six feet, graying at the temples but with a full head of thick, brown hair. He had sharp features and smooth skin. It was obvious to her that he spent time at the gym. It was impossible to accurately guess his age. He could be anywhere from late thirties to mid-fifties.

That was the kind of man she'd like in her life, timeless and ageless. She glanced at the dates on his degree and quickly did the math. He was about fifty-seven.

"Hello Mia," he said, extending his hand to greet her. He clasped her hand with both of his and held it for a moment longer than the casualness of a handshake. It was as if he needed to pause to gather his thoughts. She immediately felt a wave of dizziness come over her. She intuitively knew that his news was not going to be good.

He sat in the tufted leather chair behind his desk as if using the desk to place a physical barrier between them.

"How are you today?" he inquired warmly, leaning forward and making direct eye contact.

"I'm ok, just really afraid of what you are going to tell me," she responded. "Now it's my lower back that aches. The pain keeps moving. What's wrong?"

He took a deep breath and in an even and unemotional tone replied, "You're right, the news is not good. The results of the CAT scan confirmed what I suspected from your bloodwork the other week. It is pretty clear. You have pancreatic cancer. I want to send you to a specialist as soon as possible."

He paused for a moment to let the news sink in. Tears welled in her eyes, but she could not process the information fast enough to ask a coherent question.

"We'll need to put together a plan of attack," he continued.

He talked some more but she heard little else after hearing the word cancer. It was as if she were punched in the stomach. She was having trouble catching her breath. Tears rolled down her cheeks automatically, without having the sensation of crying.

"Pancreatic cancer is very serious, and time is really precious. Dr. Van Olsen is the oncologist I want you to see. His training was at Sloane Kettering in New York and his area of concentration is cancer of the pancreas. We're lucky to have someone with his credentials in Hartford. With your permission, I will send your file over."

He paused for a moment to allow Mia to digest this information and then continued.

"I'll make a few calls and I'd like to get you in to see him in the next day or two. He'll need you to have a biopsy done and a full series of tests run. We can't waste any time."

Dr. Barclay handed her a packet of information on cancer treatments along with appropriate contact numbers.

"I know this is frightening for you. But you have to know that Dr. Van Olsen is among the best in the country within this very specialized field. And you can feel free to call me any time you need to," he offered.

Mia walked to her car in stunned disbelief. *How could this be happening to her?* she thought. It felt like it was the beginning of a long, long nightmare. She sat in the car and wept.

Chapter Three

As Mia was sitting in her car in Dr. Barclay's parking lot, Tommy Green pulled up to the drive-up window at Fleet Bank on the other side of town. Friday was payday and he loved to cash his check at Cindi's window even though he used up most of his lunch hour getting there and back.

Tommy and Cindi had been dating on and off since his sophomore year. She was three years older and had ambitions of meeting someone who would take her far away from her East Hartford life.

Cindi graduated two years ago and, after a two-week training program, she was a junior teller. She liked working the drive-up window and interacting with the customers.

Cindi, *with an i,* as she liked to say, appeared to the world to be simple and somewhat ditsy with lots of flowing blonde hair. Knowing that she was never going to use the small college fund her parents earmarked for her education, she cashed it out and invested in a wardrobe full of fashionable clothing.

A few new push-up bras from Victoria's Secret enhanced her already ample breasts, demanding the male attention she sought.

She regularly read half a dozen magazines on style, beauty and fashion. She mimicked the gestures and language of the Glastonbury housewives who cashed checks at her teller window. She couldn't believe how much money they had.

She often daydreamed about having a Land Rover, a baby and a country club membership. That would only come if she could land the right guy.

She spent more of her money on clothes than on rent. On any given weekday night she could walk into one of the upscale bars in affluent West Hartford where she would inevitably drink for free. There was always a young executive around to buy her a drink for a few minutes of bar chatter.

If she wore one of a dozen pairs of sling back high heels, or what she referred to as *throw me down and fuck me shoes*, she was often treated to dinner as well.

She had the sense that the men she was meeting were only interested in getting her into bed. She was not the girl to be taken home to meet Mama. It frustrated her that she was not taken seriously.

She often thought about taking some classes at the community college, but never got around to it.

Having sex with Tommy was great. He was her steady weekend date. That is until something better came along. Now that she had her own apartment, a six-room flat shared with two other girls, they got to have sex as often as they wanted.

But to her, Tommy was just a passing thing. He was never getting far from here. Cindi was pretty certain that ten years from now he'd still be working on the landscaping crew, telling high school stories over beers with his buddies.

"Hey Cindi, let's hang out tonight," Tommy said as he pulled his rusting Nova up to the window. He placed his paycheck into the tray.

"Jesus, turn down the radio, I can hardly hear you."

"I was thinking about picking up a movie, a six pack and a pizza. Maybe we can light up a doobie and play *Cheerleader and the Football Captain.*"

Though she longed for a relationship with a grown man, she still loved how creative and playful he was.

"OK, big boy. Throw me your best *Hail Mary*," she said in a little girly voice that mimicked a cheer-leader.

Their laughter was interrupted with the tap of a horn from the impatient driver of a silver Lexus waiting behind him.

Glancing at the rear-view mirror, Tommy could see the vanity plate on the Lexus. "MR LAW 1" on a license plate spoke volumes about the driver.

"What an asshole," he said as he showed MR LAW 1 the middle digit of his left hand. He blew a kiss to Cindi and drove away, leaving in his wake a puff of gray smoke from the exhaust pipe of the old Chevy Nova.

Chapter Four

Andrew Paesano, Esq., pulled his Lexus up in the space vacated by Tommy.

"Cocksucker," he mumbled to himself, as he watched the Chevy Nova pull away. Being flipped off by a snotty kid who made in a year what he earned in a week wasn't bringing out the best in him.

Though Mia usually ran his errands, she had called in sick again today, so he was forced to get his own cash for the weekend, As well as pick up his own dry cleaning.

While most men his age had turned flabby in the gut, Paesano was proud he stayed trim and fit. Only a few pounds more than what he weighed when he took second place in the NCAA Squash Tournament a dozen years earlier as an undergraduate at Trinity College.

But then, he had always been a bit of an over-achiever. Three years after a near perfect score on the LSATs, he graduated from Yale Law School, second in the class.

Finishing second both at championship squash and then again at law school aggravated him to no end. Once as a child, he broke out in tears after finishing second in the school's spelling bee. Upon arriving home, he tossed his second place ribbon in the trash. How he hated not winning.

Paesano was a perfectionist, driven to succeed. He was affable, charming and quick witted. He wore heavily starched white shirts, designer labels, or custom suits, and highly polished Italian loafers. Always immaculately groomed, rarely would one find a hair out of place or a spec of lint anywhere on him.

The girls in the office referred to him as *Mr. Perfect*, never knowing that he was still bothered about losing his championship squash match. Or that it drove him crazy thinking about the B he got in his first-year tort class, thereby making it impossible to graduate first in his law class.

He dropped the check into the outstretched slot and made eye contact with the pretty blonde teller. As they exchanged smiles, he couldn't help glancing at her chest. The stirring in his loins reminded him that he hadn't gotten laid in weeks.

"Excuse me sir, but I'm going to need to see some identification before cashing this check."

She really didn't, but it was one sure way of being with him a little while longer. He was gorgeous. His car was gorgeous. And she saw no wedding band, allowing her to enjoy the fantasy of being with him.

He passed his driver's license through the window. The address told her the rest of the story. Bellingham Drive. The best street high in the Glastonbury Hills. That told her all she was curious about. That and the fact that he was 36 and there was no Mrs. on the check.

"Thank you, Mr. Paesano," She said, returning his license and the ten one-hundred-dollar bills. "Is there anything else I can do for you today?"

He glanced at the name tag on her ample chest and made a mental note of her name. Cynthia Reynolds.

"Thank you, Cynthia. You've brightened my otherwise dull day. Have a wonderful weekend."

"It's just Cindi. *Cindi with an i.* Hope to see you again. Have a great day," she chirped.

Their eyes held a momentary gaze, and they shared a brief smile. As he drove away, each of them were lost in a temporary fantasy. Hers was becoming Mrs. *MR LAW 1* and all that it entailed.

His was of her spread out on his four-poster bed for the weekend.

As he was pulling out of the bank's driveway, he saw his assistant, Mia, drive past in her easily recognizable red Camry. *She called in sick today? She doesn't look very sick to me*, he thought.

Mia pulled into the parking lot of her condominium. She saw the boys from the maintenance crew sitting on the back of the pick-up truck passing a joint.

Chapter Five

Had she not been distracted by the news from Dr. Barclay, she might have become irritated that these guys appeared to be done with their workday. They were drinking beers and smoking, horsing around as teenagers do. And it was not yet noon.

Upon further reflection, she realized she was a little jealous. To her, these guys didn't have a care in the world, while she felt the burden of her worries might crush her. She parked and went inside.

Tommy was sitting on the tailgate of the pick-up truck with his two buddies. They had been inseparable since Mrs. Pandu's fourth grade class at Silver Lane Elementary school.

Tommy, Fish and Shakespeare were best friends. Since as long as they could remember, they had been in each other's daily lives. Their camaraderie was evident in their easy banter and the way they would finish each other's sentences.

Fish's real name was Clarence Trout. The quickest way to provoke him into a fight was to call him Clarence. Fish was proud to go through life with his nickname. Sometime in junior high even his teachers began to call him Fish.

He was a happy-go-lucky character who found humor in practically everything. He went from *class clown* in elementary school to being voted *Most Likely to Be on Saturday Night Live* by his high school classmates.

Billy Williams earned the nickname Shakespeare because he read an amazing number of books. It started in the fourth grade on a dare. Over the course of that year he read every book in the Silver Lane Elementary School library. To be fair, East Hartford didn't spend much on their school libraries. But it was a large room full of books. And Shakespeare did read them all.

Now you might think that Shakespeare would look or act like some bookish nerd. Far from it. He was a tough kid with a quick temper. He walked through life with a chip on his shoulder. Often itching for a fight. And there were a lot of fights.

Earlier that week, Fish stopped into a popular hang out with his false ID. After grabbing a beer he began to chat up a pretty blonde in a UCONN sweatshirt.

How he loved the college girls. It was easy for him to fake the part of a college man. He was confident that he was too quick witted to be caught in a lie by a half-drunk college co-ed.

Just as he was going to invite her to go for a ride to look at the stars – a corny but workable line – three of her frat boy friends walked in.

"What are you doing with this sad sack of shit townie?" they demanded to know.

"He's cute and he is in school with us," her words slurred out.

The three frat boys cornered Fish, demanding to see his student ID. When he couldn't produce one, they got physical, grabbing and pushing him. Punches were thrown and Fish was pushed through the door into the parking lot. Only an ear-piercing scream from the blonde kept the frat boys from doing further harm.

Fish knew that his bruises and scrapes would heal soon enough. But it was his ego that got the brunt of the beating. Three on one. He never even got to land a punch. Twenty minutes later Fish reentered the bar. This time with Tommy and Shakespeare. All Fish had to do was point. And all hell broke loose.

Bar fights generally don't last very long. This one was no different. What was memorable though was its ferocity. Had Fish not yelled at them to stop the beating, the frat boys' next ride would have been in an ambulance. Tommy, Fish and Shakespeare left the bar and drove a few minutes to their favorite spot along the banks of the Connecticut River. They cracked open a couple of six packs and laughed about the ass-whooping they just put on those frat boys.

That's the way these boys rolled. They always had each other's backs.

Over the last few years they'd smoked their body weight in pot. And now they were the core of the landscaping crew at Georgetown Commons. The management company they worked for offered little to no supervision. So long as there were no complaints, they were pretty much left alone. They made their own schedule. Mowing, weeding, planting and mulching. Leaving plenty of time to horse around. Smoke a joint. Or drink a beer. Here it was, Friday afternoon. Time to quit work for the day, light up a doobie, and then head over to the Triple A Diner.

Chapter Six

In the heart of the town, on Main Street, sat the Triple A Diner. Like a lingering relic from another era. Neon lights flickered in the window advertising their milkshakes and burgers, inviting patrons into its warm, nostalgic embrace. The juke box offered the latest top billboard hits.

Tommy and his friends sauntered in. The Triple A Diner was their sanctuary. They always walked in with a sense of ownership, claiming their usual booth in the corner. The booth, upholstered in cracked red vinyl, had witnessed countless animated conversations, lots of laughter, and the occasional tears.

Tommy slipped into the booth first. Fish and Shakespeare slid in next, on the opposite side of the chipped formica table. The boys knew that these moments were fleeting. They were on the cusp of adulthood. Big decisions lay ahead. But for now, they had this booth and each other's company.

Mabel was a seasoned waitress, middle-aged and round in the middle. She had been here since the love of her life Charlie never made it home from Nam. That was over twenty-five years ago. Not much in her life had changed since.

"Hey boys. How are you doing tonight?" she asked as she wiped down the table.

"We're a little concerned about climate change and what will become of us when East Hartford becomes a desert," said Fish.

"Fish, you are such an idiot," Tommy and Shakespeare said simultaneously. And the three broke out in laughter.

"You guys never fail to put a smile on my face, and brighten up my dull Friday nights. So, what's it going to be, boys, the usual?" Mabel asked with a bright smile.

"Three cheeseburger specials. Along with a mountain of fries. Coke for me and my friend Shakespeare. And a chocolate milkshake for Fish," said Tommy.

In a fast-changing world full of unknowns, there was one thing in their lives they could count on besides each other. If it was Friday, they would order the cheeseburger special at the Triple A Diner.

Mabel smiled as she jotted the order on her pad. She liked these boys and hoped they would soon find a life away from here.

"So, Shakespeare, you hear back from your college applications yet?" asked Fish.

"Yeah. I am going to school down south. Everyone is so slow down there. I'll be a fucking genius. Besides, I love the sound of a southern accent coming from a pretty girl."

"Man I thought you and Becky were headed down the aisle someday," joked Tommy.

"No. This thing ends when I leave for school. We've been dating for six months. She'll let me play around with her a little. But I can't get her pants off."

"You mean she's holding her hoo-ha hostage," said Fish.

The three boys laughed hard. They loved the way Fish could spin a sentence.

"What's up with you, Fish?" Tommy asked.

"Well. I finally did it. I signed up for an open mic at the Comedy Shack. I got 10 minutes on Thursday night. I need you guys to be there. It can be a tough crowd. If you are not funny, they boo the shit out of you."

"We're in," Tommy and Shakespeare said in unison, just as the cheeseburgers arrived.

"So what about you T-man? How you doing with Cindi....*with an i*?" Shakespeare asked. "We all know that her hoo-ha has never been held hostage."

"Bite me, man! She wants out of this town even more than me. We're just biding our time. She's convinced that in 20 years I'll still be here working some shitty maintenance job. Sporting a pot belly. Without a pot to piss in or a window to throw it out of. She might be right. She wants a big house with a white picket fence. You know, and all the bullshit that comes with it. The nice car. The cushy lifestyle of the rich and the arrogant."

"Yeah, but she's still an idiot. That is *idiot with an i*. But she does have a great rack. Definitely top shelf trophy wife material," remarked Fish.

"And, Fish man, that's why I love you," said Tommy.

"Is Mr. Green still giving you a rash of shit?" asked Shakespeare.

"Not a day goes by when he doesn't hassle me. I'll turn 18 soon enough. I'll get my diploma and figure out how to get out of here. And away from him."

Chapter Seven

Mia sat in an exam room in Dr. Van Olsen's office at Hartford Hospital. True to his word, Dr. Barclay had called in a favor and gotten her an appointment surprisingly fast. She glanced around her at the bleak surroundings. The walls were painted a depressing shade of green. More like the motor vehicle department than a medical office.

"Good morning, Mia. I'm Dr. Van Olsen. Dr. Barclay is an old friend and he said to take good care of you. And that's what we are going to do."

"Thank you, doctor," Mia managed to respond. It was cold sitting there in a paper gown. Her hands were shaking, and her voice quivered. Of course, that could also be from being terrified.

Dr. Van Olsen was a much younger and shorter man than she expected. She guessed he was on her side of 40. He was thin and pale, like he hadn't seen the sun in months.

So this is what becomes of the nerdy oboe players who get shoved in their high school lockers, she thought to herself. Right now she didn't need a football star or homecoming king. She needed this guy. Who spent his life buried in books to become the highly respected physician, and who she hoped was going to save her life.

"I am sorry to tell you that I concur with Dr. Barclay. There is no doubt in my mind. The PET scan and endoscopic ultrasound are conclusive. You do have pancreatic cancer. And it is aggressive. The cancer has metastasized to your lymph nodes and possibly nearby blood vessels.

"Therefore, I want to immediately start you on a course of chemotherapy, to see if we can arrest the spread. The chemotherapy will be in combination with radiation therapy. High-energy X-rays to kill the cancer cells.

"I know this is very scary for you. I already have a team assembled, including Dr. Blenner, our gastroenterologist. Dr. Solomon, our pathologist. And Dr. Samberg, our social worker. You will meet with each of them in the coming weeks."

He paused for a moment to let Mia adjust to the news. This was the part of his job he hated the most. He knew her diagnosis did not look good. Yet he had to remain positive. It was not his job to relay a death sentence. Every so often a person with a chart this bad did go into remission.

Mia just sat there silently. Unable to move. Hardly breathing. Tears rolled down her cheeks.

"What is my prognosis?" she stammered out.

"I can't be certain right now. We'll know better after a few courses of chemo and radiation. But I can tell you that this is quite serious. And we'll do everything we can to keep you comfortable and fight this together.

My assistant, Laura, will schedule you for your first chemo treatment as soon as possible."

He put his hand on her shoulder. Their eyes held contact for a long moment. His eyes were misty too.

Chapter Eight

Most of the 100 seats in the *Comedy Shack* were filled. Though none of the patrons there remembered or cared that this was once *Pete's Bar.*

Pete's had been serving shots and beers to the construction and manufacturing trade guys since the mid-1970s. But, like most things in East Hartford, his clientele got old, moved South or died.

Pete's was run by Pete himself, head bartender, chief bottle washer, bookkeeper and boss. He wore a crusty expression with a mood to match. To even the most casual observer he had the appearance of a hostile and angry man.

He served his last drink to a largely empty bar on New Year's Eve.

His two sons found his body the next day. A heart attack ended him just after midnight.

The boys, now in their early 40s, began planning the *Comedy Shack* on the way home from Pete's funeral.

They never wanted to be in the bar business. Jim sold houses. Tim ran a small contracting firm. Neither was setting the world on fire. Now that the *old man* was gone, this could be their big break.

Three months later the *Comedy Shack* opened. It was a hit. Since East Hartford is located halfway between NY and Boston, the boys had little trouble booking B list talent. Old timers looking to make a comeback. Or upstarts working toward building a following and a career in comedy.

Thursday was their favorite night. *Open Mic Night.* It was their hope that some unknown would step onto their stage and become a rising star. An overnight sensation. The next Seinfeld.

Comedians who make it big never forget where they got their start. Jim and Tim planned to ride those coattails someday.

Tommy and Shakespeare grabbed a table up front, nursing a couple of Buds. They knew Fish was funny. But funny to them is a lot different than standing on stage trying to make people laugh.

To be sure, they would handle anyone who tried to heckle their buddy Fish.

An hour later, after sitting through an endless stream of unfunny people, eish was introduced.

He steps to the mic and looks at the audience and smiled.

"Hi. My name is Fish. (a few giggles) Listen. This is my first time on stage. My parents want me to be a lawyer. (a few more giggles) Seriously. Do I look like the guy you want to call when you get busted? I didn't think so. I wouldn't call me either.

"So do me a favor. Would you all smile? He pulled the disposable camera out of his shirt pocket and starts taking pictures. One is of him with the audience in the background. This will really piss off my parents." (laughter).

He scratched his head and continued, "So, I'm at that age where all my friends are planning their futures, and I can't even plan my meals for the week. Seriously, I can barely decide between instant ramen and mac 'n' cheese. And they're over here picking career paths like it's a fucking buffet." Fish's voice pitched louder.

"They're like, 'I'll have a little bit of engineering, a dash of law school, and can I get a side of accounting?' I'm like, 'Uh, I'll just stick with the pizza swirls.'" (louder laughter).

"I've had my own apartment for a little while now. Other than having to come up with the rent every month, my biggest challenge is cooking. Every recipe I see online is like, 'Super easy, just 15 minutes.' Then you start reading it. It's got 26 ingredients. Half of which I've never heard of. Who has saffron laying around, anyway?" (laughter)

"My spice cabinet consists of salt, pepper and disillusionment. Basil, oregano and parsley might as well be the names of Italian cities I'm never going to see." (more laughter)

When he finally finished his set, it was to cheers. He left them wanting more. More of him. It was his *aha* moment. You could see something change inside of him on stage. He felt at home up there.

"Fish, you were great! They loved you, man!"

"Thanks, Tommy. And thank you guys for being here. I was scared shitless until I saw your faces. I now know what I want to do with my life," Fish said. "Fuck college. I want to do stand-up," he added as he drained his bottle of beer.

"What was that bullshit about you having an apartment. You're 17 and live in your mother's basement," said Shakespeare.

Fish leaned forward and whispered, "Shhh. They think I'm 23. What's a little white lie in the comedy biz?"

The three friends had a celebratory shot and a couple more beers as they sat through a few more sets of stand-up. No one that night had the chops that Fish displayed. They knew he was launched.

On the drive home Tommy was lost in thought. Shakespeare would soon go off to college some- where down South. Tommy knew he was never coming back. And Fish would soon be off looking for comedy stages. God only knows where he'd end up. Meanwhile, what the hell was he going to do?

I don't know how much longer I can put up with my dad's bullshit, he thought to himself as he pulled into his driveway. Mr. Green was snoring soundly on the sofa in front of the blaring TV when Tommy walked in, tip-toeing to his room.

"Fuck Mr. Green," he quietly laughed to himself.

Chapter Nine

“Hey Mia, how are you doing? Feeling better I hope,” said Paesano, still annoyed that she called in sick the other day and he saw her driving around.

“We need to talk,” she said while entering her boss’s office.

He motioned for her to take a seat. He was on high alert. Either she found another job and was giving her notice, which would suck for him. Or she was looking for a raise. Which would suck for her. 'Cause the answer would be *no*.

“I don’t know how to say this, so I’ll just spit it out. I have been diagnosed with pancreatic cancer. They want me to start with chemo and radiation immediately. I need to take a leave of absence while I fight this thing.”

Paesano, who was usually cool and aloof, came out from behind his desk and sat in the club chair next to her. His hand gently rested on her shoulder.

The memories of losing his mother to breast cancer last year flooded back to him. He was well aware that cancer of the pancreas is as bad a diagnosis as you can get.

"Listen to me. You take off whatever time you need. With full pay and full benefits. I know sometimes it doesn't look like it, but this place is a family. And we take care of our own. I'll square it with the partners. You just take care of you. And let me know if you need anything," he added.

Mia dabbed her eyes with a tissue she brought in with her. She knew she would not be leaving his office without shedding a few tears, no matter how her conversation went. She had not expected much support, and was deeply moved at receiving it.

"Thank you so much," she sniffed. "My files are well organized. One of the other girls can step right in."

Mia walked to her desk, where she put some of her personal belongings in a box. There was a part of her that hoped she'd be back. And a part of her that feared she would not.

Walking out the door in the middle of the day carrying a box of her belongings left all who saw her to assume she was being let go.

As Paesano went to inform his partners what was happening, the staff gossip immediately began.

Mia tossed her box in the car and headed home for a good cry. Her back hurt. And she was frightened of what the future might hold.

Chapter Ten

Mia's anxiety was peaking as she walked into the chemo infusion center for her first treatment. It was a brightly painted space. Primary colors. Eye-pleasing seashore graphics.

She recognized the classical music being piped through ceiling speakers. Her first thought was Chopin. But it could also be Haydn. She smiled to herself, remembering how long it had been since she studied music history. Or for that matter, even attended a live concert. A mix of potted and hanging plants in a wide array of sizes offered some evidence that life can exist within these walls. It was in this pleasant environment where soon her body would be filled with poisons in hopes that the cancer is killed off before she is.

She carried a James Patterson novel. A simple beach read, though this was hardly a day at the beach. Still, she assumed her attention span would be limited in this environment, and simple was about all she could handle right now. The pamphlet she picked up in Dr. Van Olsen's office suggested bringing something to read, along with a light blanket and a few snacks (crackers) to help manage the dreaded side effects. She was hoping the fatigue, nausea and chills wouldn't kick in until she was back at home.

She was greeted at the front desk by an overweight, overly cheerful administrator. Since all of the necessary paperwork was completed in advance, she only had to show her health insurance card and driver's license. Mia was then escorted to the infusion area. Reclining chairs were placed around the perimeter of the large communal space. It was 10 a.m. and the place was already filled with people at various stages of treatment. The atmosphere was quiet, tinged with the hum of IV machines and soft conversations.

Mia was next met by a nurse, who explained each step of the process. She began to administer the chemotherapy through the port-a-cath, which had been surgically placed in her chest earlier in the week. Mia did her best to keep her breathing steady. She remembered her breathing exercises. Inhale for four seconds. Hold. Then gently exhale. She repeated this over and over again as the infusion began. Mia felt a cool but not unpleasant sensation as the drugs initially entered her blood-stream.

She sat there for three hours, sometimes feeling fine, at other times grappling with nausea. She had an awful metallic taste in her mouth. And then a sudden wave of extreme fatigue.The nurses kept a close eye on her for adverse reactions, ready to intervene if needed.

"That'll do it for today, Mia. You did great," the nurse said gently as she disconnected her from the machinery that had pumped life-giving poisons into her system all morning.

Mia felt a sense of relief leaving the infusion center. It went about as expected. A patient in the chair next to her told her that the first session was the easiest.

"It gets harder. This is my third round of infusions. I've been here something like a dozen times," she had confided.

"My secret to surviving this has been pot. Smoking a joint each night has helped me with pain management and nausea. You are not going to want to eat anything after these sessions. The pot will also help you with your appetite."

Mia had never smoked pot. She didn't have a clue of where to get some or how to use it. Her only guideline was to follow a strict regimen of anti-nausea medications, stay hydrated and to eat small, frequent meals.

"We'll see you back here on Wednesday," the overly cheerful lady at the desk said. Mia had an urge to punch her in the face. In one short day, her cheerfulness had become extremely irritating.

Dark clouds were forming as she got into her car. The ten-minute drive felt long. And she was momentarily confused. Pausing at a stop sign she was unsure whether to go left or right. A car beeped behind her snapping her back to attention. She made a right turn, thankfully it was correct. She was lost in her thoughts and didn't remember driving home. Yet somehow there she was, engine still running, parked in front of the door to her condo.

Mia flopped down on her sofa and flipped on the Lifetime Channel hoping to be distracted by a silly movie. She hated sports and had no patience for news. Cuddled under her favorite blanket, she fell soundly asleep.

Chapter Eleven

Mia awoke to the sounds of a lawn mower, weed whacker and leaf blower. It was 4 p.m. She had been asleep for about three hours.

She peeked through the open slit in her curtains and saw the three landscaping boys working at prettying the area outside of her home. Though she was annoyed at being awakened, she did appreciate how good a job they did, in spite of being stoned much of the time.

That gave her an idea. She opened the door. Immediately making eye contact with the tallest of the crew. She waved him over.

Tommy turned off the leaf blower. He walked over to her expecting to get blasted for making so much noise. He decided to be polite. Telling her to fuck off would result in a formal complaint. And he'd probably get fired.

"Hello," was all he said.

"Listen. I'm Mia. And I'm not sure how to ask you this," she said.

Tommy took a quick appraisal of her. She was twice his age. He'd seen her around the complex from time to time. She was still pretty but would benefit from spending a few hours with Cindi for a makeover.

"I'm Tommy. I know we're making some noise out here. I hope we didn't disturb you. But there's no way to cut grass or trim shrubs quietly."

The kid had some manners, she thought. He was a nice-looking young man who really needed a haircut. And some better friends, she observed, as she glanced over at his also shaggy landscaping buddies. Fish in his well-worn and long out of date *Y2K* hat, and Shakespeare in his FBI (female body inspector) tee shirt, were taking a smoke break as she spoke with Tommy.

"It is hot out here. Can I offer you a cold lemonade? I need your advice on something," she said. She opened the door wider, and he followed her inside.

"Nice place. I like your taste in art," he said as his eyes darted around her living room seeing a number of framed paintings and prints.

"Thank you, please have a seat. I'll grab a couple of lemonades for us," she said.

Tommy figured that if she were trying to seduce him, she'd be serving wine or cold beers. And maybe be wearing something more revealing instead of a sweatshirt. She placed the drinks on a couple of coasters on the glass coffee table. And took a seat across from him.

"OK, here it is. I've been diagnosed with cancer. And just started an aggressive chemo program this morning. It has been only one day and I'm already a mess. A woman I met this morning suggested that smoking marijuana would help me. But I have no experience with pot. I've seen you guys light up a joint a few times. And I'm kind of in trouble here. Can I buy some pot from you? And hire you to teach me how to smoke it. I'm not a narc or anything. I'm just a scared woman with cancer."

Tommy glanced down at the table and saw the pamphlet from Dr. Van Olsen's office, *Managing Your Cancer Treatment.*

"It's Mia, right? Listen, you don't have to pay me anything. I can bring a few joints over here tomorrow. I'll even let you borrow my water pipe which might be a little less harsh on your throat," he said.

"Thank you so much," she said, teary-eyed. "You are so kind. Can we just keep this to ourselves? I don't want you or me to get in any trouble."

"Sure. I'll just have to tell my buddies out there. They have been like brothers to me since we were in the fourth grade. It is either tell them the truth or let their imaginations run wild. And believe me, these guys have wild imaginations. Simple truth is best," Tommy chuckled.

She smiled along and nodded, secretly relieved, and a little in awe of what she had just asked.

Chapter Twelve

F ish and Tommy got into Shakespeare's car, an old Mustang. Tommy rode shotgun. Fish crawled into the back seat. In polite circles the twelve-year-old car would be referred to as *a beater.* The car was heavily rusted but nevertheless wore its dings and dents proudly into its old age. It got Shakespeare around town, but no one was anxious to take it on the highway as you had to pump the brakes several times in order to bring it to a full stop.

But the most annoying thing about the teenager's car was the small hole in its muffler, causing a constant noise, and forcing its passengers to speak loudly, almost shouting to be heard above the din.

"Jesus Christ, Shakespeare, you read all of these books?" Fish said as he shared the back seat with several dozen novels.

"Yes, Fish. They are the classics. The best works ever written," Shakespeare said.

"I think I can get a 10-minute set out of these," Fish said. Both Shakespeare and Tommy knew what was coming next. In his best professorial voice Fish quickly read the new and improved titles of the books grabbing each one as he comments.

"Moby's Dick. Getting Tail in Two Cities. Tequila Mockingbird. One Hundred Years of Solitaire. In Cold Bloody Marys. War and Peace of Ass and of course who could forget Brideshead Revisited or Getting a Blow Job on Your Second Honeymoon."

"Stop it Fish, you're such an idiot," the boys shouted nearly in unison, while just barely holding in their laughter.

They drove on silently. A few minutes later Shakespeare asked, "So Tommy, what's the deal with that lady at the condo? Are you hitting that?"

"No. For God's sake get your mind out of the gutter. Like I told you, she just asked me to score her some weed to help her with the side effects from the chemo treatments she's getting."

Shakespeare pulls the car over in front of Tommy's house. The noisy muffler attracted the attention of the neighborhood boys shooting hoops in the driveway across the street. And drew a disapproving look from Mrs. Sheldon tending her roses next door.

"Ya know," shouts Fish, "You might not be as big an asshole as most people think you are."

Tommy smiled broadly at his two friends and entered his house where he found his father, as usual, on the sofa, somewhere between asleep and passed out. Five empty beer cans sat on the coffee table, along with a smoldering cigarette in the nearly full ashtray.

He put out the cigarette and headed up to his room, hoping that he would be out of the house when his father eventually burned it down in one of his drunken stupors.

Chapter Thirteen

T he next evening, as planned, Tommy and Mia sat on her couch, the weed laid out in front of them. Mia was nervously clutching a mug of ginger tea. She looked fragile, her skin pale, her voice shaky, but her eyes held a glimmer of curiosity.

"You really think this could help?" she asked, glancing at the small zip lock bag on the table which contained the pot. To her it looked like dried out crap from the garden. A few twigs with withered buds attached.

Tommy nodded. "I heard weed... uh, cannabis... is used by a lot of chemo patients for nausea and appetite. It might even help you relax."

Mia bit her lip, hesitating. "I don't want to feel out of control, Tommy. I've always been... well, a bit of a control freak."

He smiled gently. "That's why we'll take it slow. The goal isn't to get high, just to take the edge off. And I'll be here the whole time."

She nodded slowly. "Alright. Let's give it a try."

Mia watched as Tommy took out a glass pipe and a package of Zig Zag rolling papers.

"I think you'll be more comfortable with the water pipe," he said. "It is simply a hookah which has been used for centuries in the Middle East. Today people just call it a bong. The pot gets burned in that small bowl attachment. The harshness of the smoke is diffused through the water in the bottom of the container. So it's much easier on your lungs."

To her, it looked more like a tall vase, just large enough to hold a rose or two. She watched as Tommy went and filled it with water. He then ground a small amount of the buds and loaded it into the pipe.

"Okay," Tommy began, "this isn't like those movies where people take giant hits and hold them in forever. That's overkill. You're just gonna take a tiny puff. Breathe it in. Then let it out. We're starting small, okay?"

Mia nodded her head slightly and shrugged her shoulders. She was as equally unsure about this process as she was excited.

"I can't believe you never smoked pot in college."

"I was afraid of getting caught and expelled. And the stoners I saw back then in college didn't look like they were having a good time. They were just wasted."

Tommy lit the pipe and Mia reached for the mouthpiece with trembling hands. She took a shallow inhale, paused, and exhaled immediately. Her face scrunched up as a small cough escaped her lips.

"That's normal," Tommy reassured her. "It can be a little harsh at first. How do you feel?"

Mia shook her head slightly. "I don't feel anything yet. Is that okay?"

"That's perfectly fine. It takes a few minutes to kick in. If you're up for it, try another little puff."

She nodded, more confidently this time, and took another small inhale.

After about ten minutes, Mia leaned back into the couch with a soft sigh. "I think... I think it's working."

"How do you feel?" Tommy asked again, watching her closely.

"Lighter," she said after a moment, her voice tinged with wonder. "The nausea isn't gone, but it's... quieter. And I don't feel as tense, like my body isn't fighting me for once."

Tommy smiled. "That's a good start. You might notice you get a little hungry soon, too. You probably should have some junk food handy in the future."

Mia's stomach growled, and they both laughed. "I can't believe this," she said. "I haven't laughed in weeks, Tommy."

As the evening went on, Mia's anxiety seemed to melt away. She chatted with Tommy about old memories, her voice growing more animated with each passing minute.

By the time Tommy packed up the waterpipe, Mia felt more like herself than she had in months. "I was so nervous about this," she admitted, "but you made it easy. Thank you."

"Anytime," Tommy said, giving her a warm hug. "I'm going to let you borrow my waterpipe. The bag of pot should last you for a while. Just promise me you'll only do this when someone's around to help, okay?"

"I have nobody in my life I feel comfortable with. Can you arrange to stop by every few days and help me out? I will certainly pay you for your time. And of course, any pot you bring. Just let me know how much. I could use your help here."

"I'd be happy to stop in on you. Any excuse to get away from my dad. He's a nightmare. But that's a story for another day. My two friends are like brothers. But they have their lives planned out. Fish, he's the shorter one, is going to try his hand at stand-up comedy. Shakespeare is going to college down South. I'm still a bit lost. I could use someone more worldly in my life. You don't have to pay me. Let's just hang out together as friends."

Mia smiled. Her eyes moistened. "I'm not that worldly. But I've been around twenty years longer than you. And I am a really good listener." Mia paused and then said "You are a good guy, Tommy. I hope you know that... I only have one question. Please tell me that your friend's real names are not Fish and Shakespeare."

"I'll never tell," said Tommy trying to keep a straight face. And they both laughed again.

Chapter Fourteen

T he next morning Shakespeare and Fish were driving to school. Tommy had told them he planned on popping in on Mia before school, so he wasn't along for the ride

"Let's grab some Dunkin' Donuts and head for the beach. I'm not in the mood for school today," Fish said, hoping that Shakespeare would go along with the idea.

"And please crank up the music to drown out the noise from your fucking muffler. Are you ever going to get that fixed? God, I hate your car."

"It's a long walk to the beach so stop bitching at me or we can still make first period," Shakespeare said.

As they pulled out of the Dunkin Donuts driveway, they saw Cindi standing across the street, in front of the Fleet Bank branch where she worked.

"Well, that is weird. I wonder if Cindi *'with an i'* needs a ride. Maybe she got fired or something," said Fish.

Suddenly a silver Lexus pulled up and the passenger door swung open. Cindi hopped in and planted a serious kiss on the lips of the driver. As the Lexus pulled out into traffic, they read the driver's vanity plate. MR LAW 1.

Together they both uttered, "Holy shit," staring into the space just vacated by MR LAW 1.

"Hey Fish, are you sure it was her?"

"Totally. I'd recognize that rack and that hair anywhere. I was hoping he might be her cousin or something. But when she put her tongue down his throat, I knew for sure. Tommy is gonna be really pissed!"

"You know we have to tell him, man. And you're going to start the conversation," said Shakespeare.

"Why am I always the bad news guy?"

"Because if he punches one of us in the face, I'd rather it be you. Fish, you are already an ugly bastard."

"Bite me, asshole. Alright. Let's go find him and rip the band-aid off. So much for the beach."

Fish reached into the Dunkin' Donuts bag. "You want jelly or cream?"

Chapter Fifteen

As Paesano drove away with Cindi, he laughed to himself. He told his office he was taking a required continuing education class to stay kosher with the County Bar Association, so he would be unreachable for the day.

Cindi shared with him that she told her nerdy branch manager that she had terrible menstrual cramps and needed to go home. She was pretty sure he was too afraid to ask for any details.

Paesano hoped that was a quality lie and that she was up for spending much of this day fulfilling that fantasy from the day he met her, rolling around on his four-poster bed.

They had been out on a couple of dates. And they really enjoyed each other's company. They seemed made for each other. He was a good-looking guy. The fact that he also had money was not a deterrent for her.

He couldn't wait to show her off at the country club. His middle-aged golf buddies would be drooling once they got a load of her.

"Hey Cindi, I never asked. How old are you anyway?" he asked.

"I just turned twenty-five," she lied without hesitation, having just turned twenty-one a month earlier.

"What about you, Andrew?" she asked. He shaved five years off the truth and told her he was thirty-one.

Liar! she thought. *He must have forgotten I saw his driver's license.* In any case, she didn't care about the age difference.

As he turned left onto Bellingham Drive, Cindi's eyes popped wide open. The houses on the street were huge, with beautifully manicured lawns. She could see swimming pools with gazebos somewhat secreted behind thickly designed landscapes.

Paesano lived on a cul-de-sac in a gated condominium community called Winthrop Estates. His lavish home was beautifully designed. Once inside, she asked him for a complete tour, telling him how much she loved interior design. Truth be told, she was looking for evidence of a wife or girlfriend. Seeing none she was happy his tour ended at his master bedroom suite.

They both knew what would happen next. Clothes soon fell onto the plush oriental carpet.

Chapter Sixteen

Tommy was a little surprised at how unaffected he was by the news that Cindi was seeing someone else. He knew his relationship with her wouldn't last much longer anyway. They had little to talk about. No dreams to share. No thoughts of the future.

All they had in common was good sex. Though she was creative and a bit wild under the sheets, he had become bored with her. She had the body of a Playboy Bunny, but she was dumb as a post.

So Cindi *with an i* would soon become just a happy memory.

He found he was spending increasingly more time with Mia. There was something about Mia that was oddly familiar. It became clearer over time.

Mia was about the same age as his mother was when she died. Tommy was only six at the time, far too young to understand that his life was about to dramatically change. His emotionally stunted father, who drank too much, was of little help. So Tommy was left alone to cry himself to sleep wondering to himself, *When is she coming back?*

With Mia, those deep feelings of both maternal connection and loss had slowly began to reemerge.

Tommy would go over to Mia's a couple of times a week and sit with her while she got stoned. Eventually he would partake, and they would get high together. Though the pot helped her manage her symptoms, she was not doing well. Mia became weaker with each passing day. She soon became thinner and gradually lost her hair. She rejected the idea of a wig, preferring a wide assortment of colorful head scarves to choose from each morning depending upon her mood.

Tommy would take her to doctor appointments and drive her to chemo treatments. She was uncomfortable driving. Through all of this she did not lose her sense of humor. Mia would tease Tommy about his hair as he was always in need of a haircut.

"Yeah, yeah, and who are you today, Yul Brynner? Or are you going for the pirate look? We're going to have to get you a hoop earring," he teased back.

"You might as well include a saber and an eyepatch, matey," she shot back with a smile.

One afternoon as they sat quietly after sharing some of Tommy's primo weed, he asked about her life before moving here and becoming a legal secretary.

"There's not much to tell. I grew up in Enfield. I never knew my dad. He deserted us. Mom worked as a secretary in the Board of Ed. She didn't have a formal education but encouraged me to explore the arts. I played the flute in the Fermi High School Band. I wasn't very good, but I liked making music with others. I was also in the poetry club. But my real love was art. A few times a year my mom took me to museums. My favorite was, and still is, the Wadsworth Atheneum in Hartford. I haven't been there in a couple of years."

"I never thought about it much, but I've never been to a museum. My dad is such an ignorant shit, who is only in love with his anger and his beer, the drunken bastard."

"Tommy, that is so sad. We should go there some time. A trip to the Atheneum will change your life," she said.

The thought of being offered his first trip to an art museum hit him with a mix of curiosity, skepticism and quiet excitement. He wondered if it would be boring, looking at a bunch of paintings on the walls. He was unsure how to even behave in a space he assumed was formal and elite. But he was open to stepping into a grown-up world, a chance to be taken seriously. *Just maybe this will be cooler than expected*, he thought to himself.

Chapter Seventeen

Mia's living room was quiet, except for the rhythmic ticking of a clock on the wall and the faint sound of leaves rustling in the wind outside the window. She sat curled up on the worn-out recliner she'd bought when she started her first job, her laptop perched precariously on her knees.

She stared blankly at the screen, the cursor blinking at the top of a half-written email to an old friend she'd not spoken with since high school. *How can I tell people who have not been in my life for years that I am sick and might not see my next birthday?* she thought to herself.

Sitting there with her high school friend's name on the screen before her brought back memories. There was so much she had loved, especially sketching and art in general. But she never devoted enough time to become any good at it. Now with time fleeting, she may never get the chance. Her body ached from the latest round of chemo, and the energy it took just to sit up felt monumental. She had once been a legal secretary, perky, sharp and quick with her words, known for catching errors that others missed. Now sketching was one of the few things she could do, at least now and then. Most of her days were spent battling cancer, and unsure if she even had the strength to rebuild the life she barely recognized. That is if she survived.

"Hey, Mia, you okay?"

The voice pulled her from her thoughts. Tommy, who had somehow taken it upon himself to become her caregiver, stood in the doorway holding a grocery bag. His eyes were kind and filled with a mix of concern and awkwardness.

"I'm fine," Mia lied, closing the laptop. "What did you bring me this time?"

Tommy grinned, setting the bag down on the counter. "Your essentials: canned soup, crackers, and that chocolate you keep pretending you don't want me to buy."

Mia smiled despite herself. "You're going to make some future roommate or wife very happy with your shopping skills."

"Or very broke," Tommy shot back. He walked over and sat on the armrest of the recliner, peering at the pile of books on the coffee table. His gaze landed on an art book Mia had borrowed from the library weeks ago. The cover was a facsimile of *The Lady of Shalott.*

"This is the one you keep looking at," Tommy said, picking up the book and flipping through its pages. He stopped at the painting, tilting his head. "Why does she look so... sad?"

"She's cursed," Mia said, tucking her blanket tighter around herself. "She's trapped in a tower, only allowed to see the world through a mirror. She spends all her time weaving what she sees into a tapestry."

Tommy frowned. "That's depressing. What happens to her?"

"She breaks the curse," Mia said, her voice soft. "One day, she sees a knight, Sir Lancelot, riding by, and something inside her snaps. She turns to look at the real world, not through the mirror, and the mirror shatters.

"She knows it's the beginning of the end of her spell, but she leaves the tower despite misgivings. She gets in a boat and sails down the river toward Camelot, but the curse takes her before she arrives."

Tommy stared at the painting for a moment longer. "So, she dies?"

"Yes," Mia said.

"Then what's the point?" Tommy asked, closing the book with a thud.

Mia sighed, her fingers tracing the edge of her blanket. "The point is that she lived. For the first time, she really *saw* the world, not just reflections of it. She made a choice to leave the safety of her tower, even if it was dangerous."

Tommy leaned forward, resting his elbows on his knees. "Do you think she knew it was going to kill her?"

"Probably," Mia said. "But she did it anyway. There's something very brave about that."

Tommy tilted his head, his brow furrowing in thought. "So, this knight, Lancelot—did he ever know about her? Did he see her or realize what she gave up?"

Mia shook her head. "Not really. When her boat floats into Camelot, the people find her lying in there, already growing cold. They read her name on a note she left, but to Lancelot, she was just a stranger. He looks at her and says she has a lovely face, and that's it."

Tommy's expression twisted in frustration. "That sucks. She gives up everything, and he doesn't even know? It feels like it was all for nothing."

Mia smiled faintly. "I used to think that too. But it's not really about Lancelot, or what he thought of her. It's about her. She chose to leave, to chase something real, even if it meant dying before she reached it."

Tommy looked at her for a long moment, his usual air of teenage indifference replaced with something deeper. "You are kind of like her, you know."

Mia let out a dry laugh. "I don't think so. She was in a boat, floating toward her destiny or whatever. I'm stuck here, trying to remain hopeful while cancer eats away at me."

"Yeah, but she didn't know how it would end," Tommy said. "She just did what she could with what she had. Just like you're doing." The words lingered in the air, heavier than either of them expected.

"You're smarter than you look, Tommy," Mia said after a moment, her voice cracking slightly.

Tommy grinned. "Don't let it get around. I've got a reputation to protect."

That evening, Mia sat at her small kitchen table with a cup of tea. She opened the art book once again to *The Lady of Shalott.* For the first time, she noticed something in the painting she had not seen before. It was the quiet determination in *The Lady's* posture.

She took note of how each small movement of the painter's brush added to the complexity of the painting's story. Mia soon came to embrace how much she had in common with *The Lady.* Each yearned to escape her own captivity. *The Lady* from her tower, and Mia from her cancer.

When Tommy came over the next day, Mia handed him a sheet of paper.

"What's this?" he asked.

"My to-do list. Let's call it a bucket list," she said with a smile. "Things to do before I kick the bucket. I need to make the most of whatever time I've got left."

Tommy nodded, tucking the paper into his pocket. "Sounds like a plan."

For the first time in months, Mia felt a flicker of hope. She wasn't in a tower, and she didn't have a boat, but she had something just as important.

Determination.

Chapter Eighteen

A few days later, Tommy pulled Mia's Camry into a parking space close to the entrance of the Wadsworth Atheneum.

The museum is located on Main Street in downtown Hartford. It is the oldest continuously operated public art museum in the country. Though he'd driven by its castle-like façade many times over the years, he'd never given much thought to the contents it held.

He glanced over at Mia, who seemingly appeared weaker by the day.

"You want me to go in and see if I can rustle you up a wheelchair?" he asked.

"What are you a cowboy? Don't ever say rustle up again," she teased him with a smile. "Thank you but I'm fine to walk around a bit. And there are benches inside if I need to sit for a while."

Mia handed the cashier her credit card and wondered if she would still be around when the Visa bill came next month.

Mia had taken a few art history classes in college. It was then that she became a lifelong museum goer, building on what her mother had started when she took her once in a while as a little girl. Alternating between Hartford's Atheneum, the Boston Museum of Fine Arts and New York's Metropolitan Museum, she had spent many happy hours wandering through the beautiful galleries over the years.

She had never properly thanked her mother for opening the world of museums to her, indeed for a long time she hadn't even realized the significance of those childhood trips. Now here she was, perhaps at the end of her life, coming full circle, and really it was thanks to her mom. She thought that bringing Tommy to his first museum would in part be payback to her mother, gone now going on a year.

Though the museum displayed a wide range of paintings, drawings, sculpture, artifacts and decorative arts, Mia was mostly interested in European art. She was drawn to the vibrant colors of the French Impressionists which evoked movement and passion within her.

Tommy appeared to be out of his element. He seemed a little lost.

"Don't worry about trying to understand any of what you see. Just stand in front of any piece that draws your attention, and feel how the painting inspires you. But Tommy, please don't touch anything," she added with a smile.

As they entered the Baroque rooms, she noticed that Tommy was drawn to the Caravaggio, one of the museum's prized possessions. He noticed how dark the painting was, lit only by a small sliver of light onto its subjects.

"Pretty impressive," she said.

They walked through the European collection which included Dalí, Miró, Monet and Magritte. He liked them. Then they stopped in front of the Picassos. Finally an artist he heard of. He thought that was pretty cool.

"Come on. I want to show you something really special," Mia said after her ten-minute rest on the bench in front of a heavily patterned Matisse she always liked. As they moved forward, Tommy glanced around, and before Mia could even point it out, he saw it. It was larger than he expected and the colors far more vibrant. *The Lady of Shallot* by William Holman Hunt.

"There are a number of paintings on this subject in museums around the world. But this is my favorite," she said.

"This is the painting on the cover of your artbook," said Tommy.

Mia nodded. "You already know the story. How the Lady's life in the tower symbolizes isolation, separated from the world. Notice how the mirror reflects the world indirectly, and how the loom is her way of interpreting it without engaging with it. See how the river symbolizes the flow of life, carrying the Lady toward her inevitable end? And finally, notice that the boat is her final means of escape. Carrying her both toward her freedom and her death." Mia spoke softly, not just because that's what you do in a museum but because she was once again struck by the symbolism herself... and how much it felt like her life right now.

After a few moments of contemplation, Tommy suddenly said, just a little too loudly, "Holy shit! I get it now. You can see the painting as visual art or something with much deeper meaning. How did you learn about all this?"

"You can read about it. Study it in school. Or just take your time and observe. There is a story behind most pieces of art. And it is often in plain sight."

They poked around the museum for an hour more, then stopped in for lunch at the café. By the time Tommy got Mia home, she was beat, barely able to walk to her front door.

After seeing Mia settled, Tommy headed home. Part way there, he had to turn the windshield wiper on full, because he was driving through a blinding deluge. He thought about how rain can wash away the old, signaling a fresh start or an emotional release, like tears from the sky. He fought back his own tears as he drove slowly home.

Chapter Nineteen

The Triple A Diner was as familiar as ever, with its red vinyl booths and the faint buzz of the jukebox in the corner. As usual, the clatter of dishes and the murmur of late-night conversations filled the air, but for Shakespeare, Fish, and Tommy it was just background noise. Usually they were here for the cheeseburger special, sharing some quips with Mabel, and ogling co-eds. It was one of the few things they could count on. Tonight, though, felt different. They were graduating from East Hartford High School tomorrow.

"Hi boys. I hear you guys are finally graduating tomorrow," said Mabel. "I'm so proud of you. I'm really going to miss you here on Friday nights. Your desserts tonight are on me in hopes that you'll get as far away from this damn town as possible. And maybe come back for a visit someday after you've made something of yourselves and washed every last bit of East Hartford off of you," she added bitterly.

"We're sure gonna miss you, Mabel. I can't imagine my Friday night without you and, of course, my cheeseburger special," Fish quipped. His ever present grin was always disarming.

Mabel's eyes dampened. She took a moment to make eye contact with each boy, and shared a nod of her head and knowing smile. *These guys will be fine,* she thought to herself.

Shakespeare leaned back in the booth, absent-mindedly picking at a fry. He glanced around at the other two, his best friends, the ones who'd been there through everything. "So," he said finally, "this is it. The last time we'll sit here as high schoolers."

Fish, seated across from him, snorted as he took a massive bite of his burger. "Man, you sound like we're never gonna see each other again. It's just high school, not the end of the world."

Tommy, sitting beside Fish, wasn't laughing. He swirled his straw in the milkshake, watching the chocolate spiral in the glass. "Still kinda feels like the end of something, though," he said quietly. "I mean, Shakespeare's off to Georgia for college, Fish's gonna be... what, the next Jerry Seinfeld? And I'm... well, I'm still here."

Shakespeare straightened in his seat, frowning. "Come on, Tommy. You've got time to figure it out. College, trade school, whatever. It doesn't have to happen overnight."

Fish nudged Tommy with his elbow, a grin spreading across his face. "Yeah, besides, the world needs guys like you. Who else is gonna keep me humble when I'm famous?"

That finally got a smile out of Tommy, though it was small. "Humble? That'll be the day."

"Hey, I'm serious!" Fish protested, though his grin didn't fade. "You'll be in the audience at my shows, front row, laughing your head off. And if I bomb, you can be the guy heckling me."

Shakespeare laughed, shaking his head. "Oh, he'd be great at that. You suck! You call that a joke? I've heard better punchlines from your mother!"

Tommy chuckled, leaning back in the booth. "Alright, alright, I'll consider it. Professional heckler. Sounds like a real stable career path."

Fish pointed a fry at Shakespeare. "Speaking of career paths, how're you feeling about Georgia? Excited? Scared shitless?"

Shakespeare hesitated, then shrugged. "A little of both, honestly. It's a whole different world down there. But, you know, I'm ready for something new."

"What if you hate it?" Tommy asked, his tone serious.

"Then I come back and figure something else out," Shakespeare replied simply. "Nothing's ever really set in stone."

Fish leaned back dramatically, throwing an arm over the back of the booth. "And if you hate it, you can always come on the road with me. We'll hit tiny comedy clubs across the country. I'll do the jokes, and you two can be my entourage."

Tommy raised an eyebrow. "Yeah, because that sounds super glamorous. Living out of a van, eating gas station snacks, and listening to your terrible jokes all day."

"Don't forget," Shakespeare added, laughing, "we'd have to watch him bomb every night."

Fish clutched his chest, pretending to be wounded. "You guys are brutal. But fine, when I'm selling out arenas, don't come crying to me for free tickets."

Tommy shook his head, a smile tugging at the corner of his lips. "Deal. But seriously though, what if I never figure out what I want to do?"

Shakespeare's expression softened. "You will, man. Maybe not tomorrow or next month, but you'll figure it out. You are so much smarter than you give yourself credit for."

Fish grinned, now pointing a fry back at him. "Yeah, and until then, you've got us. We're not going anywhere... except Shakespeare, who's ditching us for sweet tea, scorching heat and southern babes with accents."

"You're just jealous," Shakespeare shot back, smirking.

Tommy smirked as well. "I don't know. I'd take a front-row seat at one of Fish's terrible comedy gigs over southern humidity any day."

Fish spread his arms wide, laughing. "You two are the worst, and I love you for it."

"Hey Shakespeare. You ever heard of The Lady of Shalott? I saw the painting at the Atheneum last week with Mia, it was pretty cool," Tommy said.

"A painting of a lady cutting onions? What's cool about that?" Fish asked, dead serious, though he should have been joking.

"This is *Shalott*. It's a place, dopey. It's from a famous poem by Alfred, Lord Tennyson. The onion is a shallot," Shakespeare snickered, shaking his head.

Then it dawned on the boys. "Wait! YOU went to a museum? And they actually let you in?" Fish asked, as Shakespeare started laughing, picturing Tommy in his ripped jeans, slouching through the galleries, the guards on high alert.

Tommy found himself a bit irritated. "Yeah. First time. And shut up, I liked it. You think you could dig out a copy of that poem for me, Shakespeare?"

"Yeah, no problem, brother. How's Mia, anyway ....is she getting any better?" Shakespeare asked.

"No. She puts on a brave face whenever I see her, but she is getting weaker and weaker. I never thought I'd be hanging out and getting stoned with a grown lady. She's pretty cool but it really sucks that she's so sick," Tommy finished quietly.

"If it was me, there is no one in the world I'd want more than you and your weed in my corner," Shakespeare confessed.

Shakespeare then grabbed his straw, holding it up like a sword. "And now gentlemen, all for one, and one for all... that shall be our motto, shall it not?"

"Where is that from?" Fish asked.

"*The Three Musketeers*, Alexandre Dumas," Shakespeare replied.

"The Three Mouseketeers by Alexander Dumb-Ass. You are such a showoff, Shakespeare," Fish shot back.

Fish and Tommy exchanged a look and shrugged their shoulders. Then they picked up their own straws, clinking them against his. "To us!" they echoed.

For a moment, the three of them sat in comfortable silence, sipping the milkshakes and soaking in the moment. The jukebox hummed a soft Springsteen tune, and the diner seemed warmer than usual, as if it understood the weight of what this night meant.

For now, they were just three friends, in a booth they knew as well as their own homes. Tomorrow could wait.

Chapter Twenty

It was graduation day. For many, it was a time of celebration, having achieved a major milestone. One more step on a well-planned life, to include further education, a stint in the armed forces, or a job that can take you far away from this place.

For most others, graduation is more than just the end of classes. It is where childhood dreams come to die. Another step into adulthood, with forty or fifty years of working life to look forward to. And Tommy still had no idea what this milestone would mean for him.

It took more than half an hour for his classmates to line themselves up in alphabetical order under the hot June sun. They then marched solemnly to their folding seats on the football field as the East Hartford High School Band played a surprisingly good version of *Pomp and Circumstance*. Over his four years of high school, Tommy had never heard the band play.

He thought to himself that high school graduation ceremonies are like time capsules being cracked open. They are both funny and sad. Funny, because someone always trips on stage or mispronounces *cum laude*. And profoundly sad to realize those awkward kids you've known since middle school are now leaving you. This commencement ceremony was no different.

Tommy sat, sweating under his black polyester gown. Surrounded by the people he grew up with, all realizing the same thing. *Life is about to scatter us like confetti in a windstorm*, he thought to himself.

He was glad to see that Mia made it. She asked a neighbor to drive her over. She was seated one row up in the stands. He was a little surprised that his father cleaned himself up and made it there too, though he did look a little ridiculous in a worn-out Hartford Whalers hat. The Whalers hadn't played hockey in Hartford in years. They moved to North Carolina, leaving behind an empty civic center and a city full of disappointed fans.

After a welcome by the principal and introductions of too many people on too small a stage, the keynote speaker was introduced. He had a lot of titles but no real connection to the school, Tommy guessed he was their second or maybe their third choice. The speaker shuffled to the podium, squinted at his notes and then launched into a speech that somehow combined a Wikipedia entry on *success* with a passive-aggressive scolding.

"Follow your dreams, but be realistic." He paused for applause that didn't come. It was clear to everyone that he was asking the graduates to lower their expectations.

"The world is your oyster, but oysters don't hand you their pearls." *Thanks for the seafood lesson*, Tommy thought to himself. He glanced at Fish who was grinning back at him. A beach ball bounces through the crowd, eventually grabbed by a furious teacher. The speaker drones on about *bootstraps and grit*, concepts that sound like they came from a motivational poster in a military or corporate break room.

Then, mercifully, the speaker wrapped up with, "In conclusion, go out there and make us proud." His last line landed with all the weight of a wet napkin. Everyone clapped, either out of reflex or relief that this guy had finally shut up.

Four hundred and twenty names were then called alphabetically. Of his friends, Tommy was first to be called. "Thomas Aldridge Green." Upon receiving his diploma he heard Fish scream out, "Tommy boy!! We love you, man." That might be the biggest laugh Fish had gotten all year.

Twenty minutes later he heard, "Clarence Trout" and saw Fish grab his diploma and shout into the principal's mike "They call me Mr. Fish!" Once again, the audience broke into laughter.

After what seemed like cruel and unusual punishment being forced to sit in blazing sunshine, two rows of graduates with last names beginning with W began to be called. Fish and Tommy saw Shakespeare walk to the stage.

"William Williams," announced the principal.

Shakespeare was handed his diploma and took two steps toward the exit ramp where he paused, turning his back to his fellow graduates and guests. And flipped up his gown, flashing his naked back side to them, then proudly walked off the stage.

For a moment everyone was in stunned silence, at least until the band's drummer did a loud comedic *rim shot – ba dom tss!* And the crowd screamed with laughter. Even the obese mayor who for the last two hours had been profusely sweating on stage broke up in laughter.

Finally, the principal said with annoyance, "Mr. Williams will be attending school next year in Georgia, where they will surely not take kindly to shenanigans like that. Now, let us continue."

When it was over Tommy looked toward the now empty seat his father had occupied. *He must have gotten bored and left,* thought Tommy. Then he saw Mia who was still seated. He came over and she gave him a hug but turned down his invitation for lunch. She looked so frail.

"My neighbor is picking me up. So you go out with your friends, and I'll see you soon. I'm fine. And tell Mr. Shakespeare he has a lovely backside," she laughed.

Tommy couldn't have known that would be the last time he'd ever hear her laugh.

Chapter
Twenty-One

A few weeks later Tommy came by to take Mia to her appointment with Dr. Barclay. She'd been mostly seeing Dr. Van Olsen, her oncologist, for the past few months now. She felt he looked at her as a disease to manage rather than a person going through the scariest time of her life. He possessed all the warmth of a wet rag. She didn't like him.

"I'm really scared about this appointment. I don't seem to be getting any better. The fucking treatments are killing me, Tommy," she murmured.

Tommy had never heard her curse. And this was the first time he heard her so down in the dumps. He was concerned.

"Let's see what Dr. Barclay has to say. I know you like him a lot and trust him," Tommy offered.

The 10-minute ride to Dr. Barclay's office was driven in silence. There was simply nothing much to say. A part of him wanted to be upbeat and positive. But he was worried too. In a few short weeks he had seen her health decline dramatically. She could hardly climb a flight of stairs. Her arms had become thin and boney. Her face was drawn and ashen.

They entered Dr. Barclay's waiting room and were immediately escorted into his private office.

"Sit in with me, Tommy. I've got a bad feeling about this. Can you stay with me?" she asked.

"Sure, Mia," he said.

Dr. Barclay entered the office a few moments later. He ran a well-organized office and now more than ever she appreciated not being kept waiting.

"Hi Mia, it's good to see you today. I wanted to take some time to have an important conversation with you about your health and the best ways we can continue to support you moving forward," he said as he gazed at Tommy, clearly wondering who he was.

"Oh, this is Tommy Green. He has been helping me out for the last few months. He is a good friend. Anything you need to say to me you can say it in front of him," Mia said.

"As you know Mia, we've been working together to manage your illness, and Dr. Van Olsen has been closely reviewing your condition. We've reached a point where it might be beneficial to shift the focus of your care. Rather than continuing treatments that may not be as effective, we want to prioritize your comfort and quality of life to ensure you feel as supported as possible," he continued.

Mia knew what was coming next. In anticipation tears began rolling down her cheeks. She reached for a tissue on Dr. Barclay's desk and dabbed her eyes. Tommy stared straight ahead at a framed painting of a beach scene behind the doctor's desk. He wished he were there now. He had just turned eighteen but felt he still wasn't ready for these life and death adult discussions.

"One option we'd like to discuss is hospice care," Dr. Barclay said. Mia moaned audibly at the word hospice.

"Hospice is a specialized type of care designed to make sure you're as comfortable as possible. It focuses on managing symptoms, providing emotional and physical support, and helping you and your loved ones during this time. On your terms." he said.

Dr. Barclay paused to let this information set in. And then continued, "I imagine this might feel overwhelming or bring up a lot of questions and emotions. That's completely understandable. I want you to know I'm here to talk through everything with you. Hospice isn't about giving up; it's about making sure you have the care and support you need."

"So let's cut to the chase here," Mia said, her voice quivering. "I'm not going to beat this thing. Am I? How much time do I have left?"

"Mia, it is impossible to know for sure. But looking at how aggressive your cancer is, there is not much time. Maybe a month or so," he said gently.

This was the part of practicing medicine he hated. Bringing some difficult news was one thing. But this was a death sentence. He struggled to continue.

"This decision isn't one you have to make right now. And you're not alone in this. Dr. Van Olsen and our whole team will be with you every step of the way, helping you transition into this new phase of care if and when you're ready.

"Should you have any questions or worries you'd like to share, please know that we're here to listen and provide any information or guidance you may need."

Tommy drove Mia home in stunned silence. Dr. Barclay's words rolled around in his head leaving him speechless and numb. He wished he was wiser and could say something comforting. But the words wouldn't come.

Mia just stared out the car window noticing the azaleas and roses in their full summer bloom. As her eyes once again filled with tears, she wondered if she would outlast the flowers.

All things die, she thought to herself. *Dying at 70 is sad. But being dead before 40 is fucking tragic.*

Chapter Twenty-Two

Tommy, Fish and Shakespeare had just finished mowing the lawn and pruning the bushes around building #4. Mia's building. Graduation was now in their rear view. Nothing but sunshine and outdoor work around the condo complex was planned for this summer, while they waited around for the next chapter in their lives.

"Hey, let's take a smoke break," said Fish, always the first one of the three to ask for a break.

The three hopped up onto the tailgate of the condo association's ten-year-old Ford pickup. Tommy grabbed his Marlboro red box from his shirt pocket and pulled out two cigarettes. One for Shakespeare and one for him. They lit up.

"How about one for me, man?" Fish said.

"Fish, you've been bumming cigarettes since middle school. Don't you ever buy a pack?" Tommy said, shaking his head as he tossed the pack to him.

"Stop busting my balls. I'm saving for my year on the road hitting comedy clubs. I'm planning to give my notice in a few weeks and start my adventure at the end of July," Fish said. "Last night I got a list off the internet of 500 comedy clubs between here and the West Coast. I expect to be famous by the time I hit LA."

"You are the most overconfident person I know," said Shakespeare. "But what are you going to do for money until fame hits?"

"Got it covered, man. My parents set aside some money for college for me. Between hitting that, couch surfing where I can, and picking up some part-time work, I should be okay for most of the year," he said.

"When are you out of here, Shakespeare?" Fish asked.

"I'm going to drive down South next month and get settled in. Classes start the second week in August. I'm pretty jacked up about it."

"Hey Tommy. You're pretty quiet. Are you bummed out that we'll both be out of here soon?" Fish said.

"Yeah, kind of. You guys both have your shit to-gether. You know, a real plan for the next part of your life. And that's great. I'm sitting here kind of lost and clueless. For now I'm still Mia's weed guy. She's going through a lot of shit and not doing so well. She's kind of a wreck,"

Tommy sighed as he lit up another Marlboro. "We met with her doctor the other day. He wants to put her in hospice. That's the end of the road, man. There's no coming back from that," he added.

They sat in silence for a few moments and then Tommy says, "Nobody in my life has died. At least not that I remember. I don't really remember much about my mom. She died when I was five or maybe six. And that prick, Mr. Green, has done nothing to keep her memory alive..." his voice trailed off in sadness.

After a few minutes of silence, each of them lost in their own heads, Shakespeare asked, "So what is Mia going to do?"

"Beats the crap out of me," said Tommy, as he exhaled the smoke from his lungs and crushed out his cigarette butt on the tailgate.

"I'm so sorry, Tommy. That sucks for her and for you," Shakespeare said as he reached into his pock-et and pulled out a book of Tennyson's poems.

"Here's that poem you asked me to find for you. Alfred, Lord Tennyson is some pretty heady stuff. Let me know if you want me to explain any of it to you."

Tommy took the book and said, "Thanks. I'm going to check up on her now. Would you guys finish up? I'm taking off early today."

Chapter Twenty-Three

Tommy knocked and entered Mia's condo. She almost never locked her door.

"Mia," he shouted into the quiet living room, "It's me. Just checking up on you."

The whistle of the kettle on the stove caught his attention as he heard her muffled sob.

Tommy entered the kitchen as Mia dried her eyes with a tissue. In her best formal British accent she said, "Fancy a cuppa?"

They both smiled. Mia loved watching English movies. Tommy wasn't a fan but they both enjoyed a good chuckle every time one of the actors, faced with a difficulty, simply says, *fancy a cuppa*, as if a cup of hot tea could solve any problem. Mia poured them each a cup of hot tea. Tommy took two sugars and an amount of milk sufficient to color his tea light beige. Mia liked her tea strong, often adding his used tea bag to her brewing cup.

"I've thought about it, and I think I need to move to the hospice as Dr. Barclay suggested. I can't take care of myself here alone anymore. Will you take me over there when it's time?"

"Sure," he said.

They sat in silence for a few minutes, each lost in their own thoughts. To Tommy there was a finality to her decision. Her "moving into this next phase" also meant losing the friendship that was so meaningful to him.

Asking Tommy to take her to hospice was harder than Mia expected. She cared deeply for this young man and knew he would struggle accepting her decision to enter hospice.

Mia shakily placed her teacup back on the saucer and leaned forward with her hands in her lap. In a serious tone she said, "You've been a great friend to me these last few months. I don't know what I would have done without you. I know you are having a terrible time living with your father. I want you to move in here and look after my place. I can't leave it empty, and you need a place to live. No charge. Just take care of my plants. You'll be doing me a huge favor. My boss will prepare a lease, so it is all kosher legally. You're 18 now. If you are ready to get on with your life, here's your chance," she added.

Mia saw Tommy freeze, so she tried to lighten the moment. "Besides, your commute will be shorter," she said as they both smiled.

"I don't know, Mia," Tommy said. "This doesn't feel right to me. I mean we're not related or any-thing."

"This is my decision. I cannot think of anyone who would benefit more from this than you. I have no one. I'll call my boss, Attorney Paesano. And he'll work out all the details."

Tommy squirmed and opened his mouth to protest, but then Mia said, "I'm doing this because I want to help you. Now shut up and say thank you."

"How can I say thank you if I shut up?" Tommy retorted. But thankful he was. If only this gift didn't come at such a price.

Chapter Twenty-Four

Andrew Paesano slid his silver Lexus into an open space in the visitor parking lot in front of Mia's building. He sat for a moment trying to compose himself. Mia had asked him to stop by to discuss a legal matter. She did not have the strength to come back into the office. He assumed that she also didn't want her former co-workers buzzing around, peppering her with questions.

Paesano remembered how his mother looked in the latter stages of breast cancer last year. He shuddered as that memory of loss continued to seep into his head at unexpected and uninvited times. He grabbed his leather portfolio and a box of Mia's favorite muffins fresh from Milton's Bakery and stepped out of the car.

A few neighbors were out walking their dogs. And as usual, sharing the local gossip.

"Look at that. He is so yummy," Zelda Zimowitz said looking over the top of her oversized gold rimmed sunglasses. "He looks like he belongs in the window display at one of those fancy department store windows."

Irene Silver's toy poodle tugged on its leash pulling her out of her fantasy as she watched Paesano walk up the path to Mia's front door. "I haven't seen Mia out recently. Only that maintenance guy coming and going at all hours," she said as they walked off.

Paesano knocked on the door and waited. A quick glance at his Rolex told him he was right on time.

A moment later, the door creaked open slowly. It was shocking to see her. In just a few months she had lost a significant amount of weight. Now, her clothes were baggy. Her exposed arms appeared alarmingly thin, and her cheeks sunken on her pale face. A brightly colored bandana covered her head which he knew was hairless. They briefly embraced and she invited him in.

"I know I look like shit. But that is how I feel most days. This chemo is beating the hell out of me," Mia said as they took seats in her living room.

"I brought you blueberry muffins from Milton's. I remembered they were your favorite," he said. "I've been a lousy friend. I haven't been here to visit and I'm sorry."

"No worries. I wouldn't have been very good company anyway," she said. "Bring me up to date on the office gossip," Mia said, hoping he'd offer something to distract her.

Before he could begin, she added, "By the way *you* are looking great. You know the girls in the office call you *Mr. Perfect* behind your back? You never have a hair out of place," They both smiled.

"But you look a little different to me today. Lighter. Happier. What's going on, are you seeing someone?" she asked.

"Yes. I've been dating a woman named Cindi and I'm happier than I have been in some time," he admitted.

"That's great. You deserve to be happy," Mia said.

Mia then went on to explain that she needed a will, leaving everything to her friend, Tommy. Also, since she would be in hospice soon, she wanted Tommy to live here. She would need a short form lease so there would be no misunderstanding. She didn't want him getting jammed up with the home-owner's association. She shared with Paesano how important Tommy had become in her life, and confided a little about his personal situation.

"He needs a fresh start on what has been a shitty family situation. And I am able to give that to him," she said as emphatically as her limited energy would let her.

"Listen Mia. I'm your boss. Your friend, and your attorney. We've known each other for a long time. So I have to ask. Are you absolutely certain this kid is not taking advantage of you?" Paesano asked.

"One hundred percent. He is a good guy. And I need your help. Please do this for me," she pleaded.

Paesano nodded his head and said, "Okay. Thank you for trusting me to handle this."

Switching into professional mode, he then asked her for Tommy's full name and contact information, as well as a rough list of her assets. He said he'd prepare the will and make the lease for a minimal rental amount in order to make it a legal document.

"I'll draw up the paperwork and have it ready for you in a few days," Paesano said as his eyes moistened. "This is my cell phone number. You are priority one, Mia," he added as his voice cracked.

She walked him to the door. And they embraced. She could feel him holding back his tears so as not to upset her. This warmed her heart. He was a good man. And she could tell he cared about her.

Chapter Twenty-Five

The following week, Mia pressed her forehead against the cool glass of the car window, watching the sunny world blur as Tommy drove. The streets were familiar, yet they felt more distant now, like shadows of a life she was slowly leaving behind. Though the news of her terminal cancer had come some months earlier, it wasn't until last week that her doctor had uttered the words: *"Hospice might be the best option now."* Mia was about to cross a threshold she had never in her life fathomed reaching so soon.

The hospice facility was nestled on the edge of town, surrounded by sprawling oaks and a garden filled with various colored wildflowers. Tommy parked, and they sat in silence for a moment.

"You sure you want to do this? You could have someone come to your home. And I'd be happy to continue to help out," Tommy said softly, gripping the steering wheel tightly as if it were the only thing holding him together.

"I know. But this is best," Mia replied, though the truth was, she knew that she had no other options.

The hospice nurse, a woman named June, greeted them with a warm smile. "Welcome, Mia," she said, her voice as soothing as a lullaby. "Let's get you settled."

The room was nothing like a hospital. Soft, earthy tones gave it a homey feel, and the window overlooked the garden. A quilt patterned with sunflowers lay on the bed, and a small vase of lavender sat on the nightstand. Mia appreciated the effort to make it feel less clinical, though the ache of reality lingered.

Tommy carried in a small bag of Mia's belongings; her sketchbook, a few framed pictures, a Ken Follett novel she was sure she'd never finish and a well-worn art book containing Hunt's *The Lady of Shallot*. Mia sank into the recliner by the window. She watched a butterfly flit from flower to flower in the garden below.

The days passed in a strange rhythm. Nurses and aides came and went, managing her pain and ensuring she was comfortable. Mia often sat by the window, her sketchbook open, trying to capture fleeting moments of beauty. The play of sunlight on the garden. The curve of a nurse's smile.

Her hospice room was quiet, except for the whispering hum of an oxygen machine. When she wasn't sitting by the window, Mia lay propped against a mountain of pillows, her thin frame swaddled in a floral blanket. The soft morning light filtered through the window, casting patterns on the walls.

Today there was a knock at the door, and before Mia could answer, Tommy stepped inside. At 18, he looked older than his years, his broad shoulders and calloused hands a testament to his physical work. She no longer thought of him simply as one of the boys on the landscape crew at her condo. Now in some ways he was like the son she would never have.

She recalled how Tommy and his two buddies in their last year of high school joyously mowed, pruned and painted, seemingly without a care in the world. It took a while for her to recognize that her annoyance at their free spirits was a result of her envy. She had wished she could be more like them. And now somehow Tommy had become her friend. Perhaps her closest friend.

"Hey," he said, his voice quiet but warm. He held up a paper bag. "I brought muffins. The good kind. Blueberry."

Mia's lips curved into a small smile. "You're spoiling me, Tommy."

"Someone has to," he replied, setting the bag on the bedside table. He dragged a chair closer to her bed and sat down, his long legs stretching out awkwardly.

Now, sitting in the hospice room, Tommy looked around. "This place is nice," he said. "Comfier than I thought it'd be."

"They try," Mia replied. "But it's not home." Her voice was softer now, her energy ebbing, but she still spoke with the same frankness he'd come to admire.

Over the next few weeks, Tommy became a regular presence. He'd bring her favorite tea or muffins, sit with Mia while she napped. They smiled over old memories, cried when the weight of the situation was too much, and found comfort in their easy companionship.

Mia lay back against the pillows in her hospice bed, watching as the late morning sun spilled across the room. Her body felt heavy, each movement an effort, but her mind remained sharp, alert to the life that buzzed around her. Nurses still came and went with quiet efficiency, adjusting medications, checking vitals, and offering warm smiles.

She looked forward to hearing Tommy's soft knock on the door. Tommy wasn't just a visitor. He had become part of Mia's life in a way neither of them had expected. Against all odds, Tommy had become her only family.

He seemed to have appeared out of nowhere to help. She reminded herself that it had been her who approached him one afternoon to ask if he could find her some marijuana. She still marveled at the fact that, without hesitation, he had said "yes." And for some reason, from that day on, that awkward, loud punk of a teenage boy kept showing up, offering to run errands or cook simple dinners.

What Mia didn't know, though she may have suspected, was that she was filling a void for Tommy too. His dad was no good. Everyone knew that. And while at some point he had confided in her about the early loss of his mom, she never pictured herself filling that role. Yet, here they were, bonded in the most unexpected way.

"I don't want to be a burden," she'd told him one evening, embarrassed by how much she was leaning on him.

He set the bag and thermos on the nightstand and pulled up a chair by her bed. "How're you doing today?" he asked, his voice gentle.

Mia shrugged. "The same," she said, her voice raspy but steady. "Tired. But I'm here."

Tommy nodded, understanding. He didn't push her to elaborate. Instead, he leaned back in the chair, and reached for the book of poems from his backpack.

"Do you remember the day we went to the Atheneum in Hartford? It was my first trip to a museum," said Tommy.

"That was a great day. I shared with you my favorite piece of art," Mia said.

"*The Lady of Shallot*," they said in unison with broad smiles.

"I've got something for you. I asked my buddy Shakespeare to find me a copy of the Tennyson poem, *The Lady of Shallot*. He explained the poem to me like you explained the painting we saw that day. /

"Jesus, it is long. That guy Tennyson used an awful lot of words to tell his story. But one section really made an impression on me. And I thought of you. Can I read it to you?" he said as he leafed through the book to a paperclipped page.

"Sure. I would like that very much," she said, as she moved the box of Kleenex from the side table to her bed, knowing that her tears would soon follow.

Tommy cleared his throat and took a sip of water, not sure at all if he could read this aloud to her.

With a steady stony glance—
Like some bold seer in a trance,
Beholding all his own mischance,
Mute, with a glassy countenance—
  She look'd down to Camelot.
It was the closing of the day:
She loos'd the chain, and down she lay;
The broad stream bore her far away,
  The Lady of Shalott.

Mia blinked back tears, reaching out to squeeze his hand. "You're a good man, Tommy. The world needs more people like you."

As the days in hospice passed, Tommy visited almost daily, sometimes twice a day. He brought little things to brighten her room – a new sketchpad and colored pencils, flowers, a playlist on his iPod of her favorite songs. They spent hours talking about everything and nothing.

Mia shared more stories about her life and the dreams she'd had for the future. Tommy, in turn, opened up about his struggles in school, the difficulties with his father and his thoughts of maybe going to community college in the fall.

"You're going to do great things," she told him one afternoon. "You've already done more for me than most people would."

"You've done a lot for me too," he said quietly. "You've shown me how to care about people. Really care."

Before he left that evening, she handed him one of her sketches - a drawing she'd done of the two of them sitting on her porch, talking the way they had so often over the past year.

"This is for you," she said. "To remind you of how much you've meant to me."

For Tommy, the time he'd spent with Mia was a lesson in compassion, resilience, and the power of human connection. And for Mia, Tommy had been a reminder that even in her most challenging moments, she was not alone.

Their friendship, forged in the foreshadow of loss, had become a testament to the beauty of showing up when it mattered most.

Chapter Twenty-Six

Tommy pulled Mia's red Camry up to his house in East Hartford. Fish and Shakespeare were left to finish up mulching some landscape beds. He took off early and they covered for him. He was lucky to have such supportive friends who knew how difficult a time Tommy was having. With summer ending, he was about to be alone to figure out his life plan.

Tommy hadn't been home in a while. A typical day for him was maintenance work. Then a few hours with Mia at hospice. And finally a fitful night's sleep in Mia's condo. It was weird for him to be in her space without her there. He hoped in time it would feel more like home. He shut off the engine and sat for a moment gathering his strength before walking into the only home he had ever known, hoping to avoid a confrontation with his father.

"Where in the hell have you been?" snarled Mr. Green, still wearing his stained and yellowed tee shirt. "You haven't been here in days. What'd you do, steal that lady's car. Or are you shacking up with her?"

Tommy was tired and emotionally drained. He didn't have the energy to get into an argument with his father, who by this time of day was well into his cups.

"She is in hospice and dying soon. I'm moving into her place. I just came home for some more of my things," Tommy mumbled.

"You stupid bastard. They are going to fucking arrest you," Mr. Green shouted, as he poked Tommy in the chest to make his point.

"Just because some lady lets you bone her doesn't mean you can steal her shit. Now help me clean this place up. The lawn needs mowing."

"Mow it yourself. I've had enough. I'm 18 and I'm out of here. And you, Aldridge Green, are an asshole!"

Mr. Green took a wild swing at Tommy's head. Tommy ducked, leaving Mr. Green momentarily off balance with his hands down. A lifetime of rage was channeled into Tommy's clenched fist. His most prominent memory was the physical and emotional abuse heaped upon him by his deadbeat father. But no more.

Tommy reared back and unloaded a ferocious punch with all of his might, directly into his father's face. He watched as his dad's knees buckled and he went down with a thud knocking over the coffee table, scattering the empty beer cans. The man was out cold.

After gathering his stuff, Tommy quickly walked back out through the broken screen door. He never looked back.

Tommy didn't know what to feel as he started up Mia's car. But he was certain Mia would help him sort out his confused feelings around having just knocked out the bully who made his life miserable.

He headed over to the hospice. It was dinner time. And Mia would be waiting.

Chapter Twenty-Seven

When Mia passed, it was gentle, like a candle's flame flickering out. She left behind her sketches, her memories, and a profound impact on the few who had shared her journey. And for Mia, her final chapter was not just an ending, but a story of love, connection, and finding beauty even in the closing of the day.

For Tommy, it was a closing of a chapter too, but in so many ways, just the beginning of a new novel. One he was thought he wasn't ready for, but with Mia's love and support, he would find a way forward. But first, he had to get through the next moments.

Chapter Twenty-Eight

Tommy was greeted at the front door by June. Of all the hospice nurses, she was his favorite. June was a middle-aged woman with kind eyes and a soothing voice that had carried too much practice in delivering bad news.

She hesitated, her fingers gripping the clipboard she held, as though the weight of it could anchor her in the moment. She directed him to join her in a small office next to the entrance. They sat in comfortable wing chairs across from each other.

"Tommy," she said softly. Her voice was tender but firm, like someone trying to soften the blow of a wrecking ball.

He glanced at her, his heart already sinking. He didn't need her to speak to know what was coming, but some part of him clung desperately to hope.

"I'm so sorry, sweetheart," June continued, her blue eyes glistening. "Mia passed away earlier this morning."

The words hit him like a punch to the gut. His breath caught, and for a moment, he couldn't tell if his chest was burning from holding it in or breaking apart. And in that small, sterile room, Tommy's world shattered.

"No," he whispered, his voice cracking as he shook his head, as if sheer denial could undo the truth. "No, she was — she was fine yesterday. She smiled at me."

"I know," June said, her voice trembling now. "She fought so hard, Tommy. She cared about you so much."

He felt tears spill from his eyes, but he didn't bother to wipe them away. His fists clenched, knuckles white. "She wasn't supposed to go yet," he choked out. "She — she promised me she'd be here. She promised."

The nurse reached out, placing a gentle hand on his knee. "Mia loved you like family. She held on for as long as she could, for you. But sometimes, the body... it just can't keep up."

Tommy's shoulders shook as sobs wracked his frame. He pressed his palms into his eyes, as if he could push the pain back inside. The silence that followed was heavy, punctuated only by the sound of his grief filling the small room.

He thought of Mia's laugh, the way it always lit up the dimmest days. He thought of her stories, her wisdom, her relentless support. And now she was gone, leaving a void so vast it threatened to swallow him whole.

"She was all I had," he whispered, his voice barely audible.

The nurse stayed by his side, silent now, her presence a quiet offer of comfort in a moment that felt unbearably empty.

After a time, June broke her supportive silence. "Tommy, Mia knew her time was short. She asked me to hold this letter for you until she passed," And she handed him Mia's letter.

Dear Tommy,

As I sit here with my thoughts flowing through me like a gentle stream, I find myself drawn to the task of writing this letter to you. It is not easy, but I want you to know how much your friendship has meant to me.

From the first day we met, I felt a connection that transcended the ordinary. Your kindness, your laughter, and your unwavering support have been my anchor in the turbulent seas of these past months.

Your presence has brought warmth and comfort to the last of my days. And for that, I am eternally grateful.

Though my journey has come to an end, I want you to know that I am at peace. Please don't mourn my passing for too long. Instead, celebrate the beautiful moments we shared.

Life will go on. And I want you to continue living it to the fullest.

To that end, I want to help you to pursue your dreams. As you know, I have no family. It was only you who showed me so much kindness over the last few months. Asking for nothing but friendship in return.

I don't have much, but I do own my condo and my Camry. And I have $38,000 in my retirement account. I prepared a will a few weeks ago. I am leaving everything I have to you.

Call my boss, Andrew Paesano at Coleman, Terrance and Paesano in Hartford. He is my executor and will handle all of the details. He'll be expecting your call.

You need to get away from your father. He is poisonous. Move into my condo permanently. Enroll in school. I know your high school grades are not great, but they will take you at the community college. It is a start. You are much smarter than you think. Go and start fresh.

You have a heart of gold, and the world is a better place with you in it.

Thank you for being the friend I needed.

I leave you with a heart full of love. Go and be the man I know you can be.

Much love always,
Mia

Epilogue

Cindi *with an i* is no more. She is now Cynthia. Or as she loves to remind people — Mrs. Andrew Paesano, Esq.

They have been married for a dozen years, and have twin nine-year-old girls, and a fourteen room home in the Glastonbury Hills. They also have a country club membership where they are the reigning pickle ball doubles champions.

The *MR LAW 1* license plate now hangs on a wall inside their three-car garage as Andrew's law partners had deemed it too gauche for their practice.

Shakespeare received a Master of Arts degree in Literature from the University of Georgia. He now is a tenured and very popular professor in their English department. He is now called Will Williams. He lives in suburban Athens with his wife and three boys Milton, Ernest and Dante.

No one there knows that he went by the name of Shakespeare as a younger man. The video clip of him mooning his high school graduation twenty years earlier continues to go viral each June. If one listens carefully you can hear the audience shouting, *"Shakespeare."*

Fish left East Hartford the summer he turned 18. It took two years of honing his comedic chops at small comedy clubs for him to make it all the way across the country. When he finally arrived in LA he was a seasoned pro. His material was fresh and honest. And he knew how to work an audience.

He now performs on the college circuit and sells out larger clubs. Like Cher and Madonna, he is known to the world by only one name. Fish.

Tommy enrolled at community college the fall after Mia Childs died. He performed well and for the first time in his life enjoyed school. Within a year he transferred to the school of real estate at the University of Connecticut. It was there he met a cute education major named Julie. They were married a few weeks after graduation. They now live in Natick, MA with their daughter Mia, and a big fluffy dog named Shakespeare.

As luck would have it, Julie's father is a real estate developer. He is delighted to have Tommy work with him. Tommy is like the son he never had.

And Julie's dad is like the father Tommy had always wished for.

Tommy's Boston office is on a high floor at International Place. It is tastefully decorated with high end furnishings. From his floor to ceiling windows is a view of Boston Harbor and Logan Airport. But his most precious possession is the framed print of *The Lady of Shalott* which hangs on the wall behind his desk. It reminds him each morning of the lady who gave meaning to his life.

Tommy, Fish and Will (Shakespeare) remain in touch through regular emails, texts, phone calls and social media posts. When they do find themselves together, it is always in a corner booth of an all-night diner sharing laughs and having the cheeseburger special.

The Lady of Shalott

William Holman Hunt, Oil on canvas, Wadsworth Atheneum Museum of Art, Hartford, CT.

The Lady of Shalott

By Alfred, Lord Tennyson, 1832

Part I

On either side the river lie
Long fields of barley and of rye
That clothe the wold and meet the sky;
And thro' the field the road runs by
   To many-tower'd Camelot;
The yellow-leaved waterlily
The green-sheathed daffodilly
Tremble in the water chilly
   Round about Shalott.

Willows whiten, aspens shiver.
The sunbeam showers break and quiver
In the stream that runneth ever
By the island in the river
   Flowing down to Camelot.
Four gray walls, and four gray towers

Overlook a space of flowers,
And the silent isle imbowers
   The Lady of Shalott.

Underneath the bearded barley,
The reaper, reaping late and early,
Hears her ever chanting cheerly,
Like an angel, singing clearly,
   O'er the stream of Camelot.
Piling the sheaves in furrows airy,
Beneath the moon, the reaper weary
Listening whispers, ' 'Tis the fairy,
   Lady of Shalott.'

The little isle is all inrail'd
With a rose-fence, and overtrail'd
With roses: by the marge unhail'd
The shallop flitteth silken sail'd,
   Skimming down to Camelot.
A pearl garland winds her head:
She leaneth on a velvet bed,
Full royally apparelled,
   The Lady of Shalott.

Part II

No time hath she to sport and play:

A charmed web she weaves alway.
A curse is on her, if she stay
Her weaving, either night or day,
*   To look down to Camelot.*
She knows not what the curse may be;
Therefore she weaveth steadily,
Therefore no other care hath she,
*   The Lady of Shalott.*

She lives with little joy or fear.
Over the water, running near,
The sheepbell tinkles in her ear.
Before her hangs a mirror clear,
*   Reflecting tower'd Camelot.*
And as the mazy web she whirls,
She sees the surly village churls,
And the red cloaks of market girls
*   Pass onward from Shalott.*

Sometimes a troop of damsels glad,
An abbot on an ambling pad,
Sometimes a curly shepherd lad,
Or long-hair'd page in crimson clad,
*   Goes by to tower'd Camelot:*
And sometimes thro' the mirror blue
The knights come riding two and two:
She hath no loyal knight and true,

The Lady of Shalott.

But in her web she still delights
To weave the mirror's magic sights,
For often thro' the silent nights
A funeral, with plumes and lights
*   And music, came from Camelot:*
Or when the moon was overhead
Came two young lovers lately wed;
'I am half sick of shadows,' said
*   The Lady of Shalott.*

Part III

*   A bow-shot from her bower-eaves,*
He rode between the barley-sheaves,
The sun came dazzling thro' the leaves,
And flam'd upon the brazen greaves
*   Of bold Sir Lancelot.*
A red-cross knight for ever kneel'd
To a lady in his shield,
That sparkled on the yellow field,
*   Beside remote Shalott.*

The gemmy bridle glitter'd free,
Like to some branch of stars we see

Hung in the golden Galaxy.
The bridle bells rang merrily
  As he rode down from Camelot:
And from his blazon'd baldric slung
A mighty silver bugle hung,
And as he rode his armour rung,
    Beside remote Shalott.

All in the blue unclouded weather
Thick-jewell'd shone the saddle-leather,
The helmet and the helmet-feather
Burn'd like one burning flame together,
  As he rode down from Camelot.
As often thro' the purple night,
Below the starry clusters bright,
Some bearded meteor, trailing light,
    Moves over green Shalott.

His broad clear brow in sunlight glow'd;
On burnish'd hooves his war-horse trode;
From underneath his helmet flow'd
His coal-black curls as on he rode,
  As he rode down from Camelot.
From the bank and from the river
He flash'd into the crystal mirror,
'Tirra lirra, tirra lirra:'

Sang Sir Lancelot.

She left the web, she left the loom
She made three paces thro' the room
She saw the water-flower bloom,
She saw the helmet and the plume,
   She look'd down to Camelot.
Out flew the web and floated wide;
The mirror crack'd from side to side;
'The curse is come upon me,' cried
   The Lady of Shalott.

Part IV

   In the stormy east-wind straining,
The pale yellow woods were waning,
The broad stream in his banks complaining,
Heavily the low sky raining
   Over tower'd Camelot;
Outside the isle a shallow boat
Beneath a willow lay afloat,
Below the carven stern she wrote,
   The Lady of Shalott.

A cloudwhite crown of pearl she dight,
All raimented in snowy white

That loosely flew (her zone in sight
Clasp'd with one blinding diamond bright)
*   Her wide eyes fix'd on Camelot,*
Though the squally east-wind keenly
Blew, with folded arms serenely
By the water stood the queenly
*   Lady of Shalott.*

With a steady stony glance—
Like some bold seer in a trance,
Beholding all his own mischance,
Mute, with a glassy countenance—
*   She look'd down to Camelot.*
It was the closing of the day:
She loos'd the chain, and down she lay;
The broad stream bore her far away,
*   The Lady of Shalott.*

As when to sailors while they roam,
By creeks and outfalls far from home,
Rising and dropping with the foam,
From dying swans wild warblings come,
*   Blown shoreward; so to Camelot*
Still as the boathead wound along
The willowy hills and fields among,
They heard her chanting her deathsong,

The Lady of Shalott.

A longdrawn carol, mournful, holy,
She chanted loudly, chanted lowly,
Till her eyes were darken'd wholly,
And her smooth face sharpen'd slowly,
  Turn'd to tower'd Camelot:
For ere she reach'd upon the tide
The first house by the water-side,
Singing in her song she died,
  The Lady of Shalott.

Under tower and balcony,
By garden wall and gallery,
A pale, pale corpse she floated by,
Dead cold, between the houses high,
  Dead into tower'd Camelot.
Knight and burgher, lord and dame,
To the planked wharfage came:
Below the stern they read her name,
  The Lady of Shalott.

They cross'd themselves, their stars they blest,
Knight, minstrel, abbot, squire, and guest.
There lay a parchment on her breast,
That puzzled more than all the rest,

> *The well fed wits at Camelot.*
> *'The web was woven curiously,*
> *The charm is broken utterly,*
> *Draw near and fear not,—this is I,*
> *   The Lady of Shalott.*

Acknowledgements

My heartfelt thank you to my wife, Norma who helped me to turn my often-scattered thoughts into a book I can be proud of. It was her idea to incorporate *The Lady of Shallot* into the storyline.

I am indebted to Colleen Brunetti of Bannon River Books who skillfully edited and designed the interior of the book, brought my manuscript to life and helped navigate the world of self-publishing.

My warmest thank you to Arlene Soto of Intricate Designs whose artistic hands once again proved that you can indeed judge a book by its cover.

A special thank you to Hartford's Wadsworth Atheneum Museum of Art for allowing me to use William Holman Hunt's painting, *The Lady of Shallot.*

Finally, my deepest appreciation to my team of beta readers who read early versions of this book. Thank you to Mark Briggs, Penny Gitberg, Vicki Gaudette, Andy Litsky, Geno Paesano, and Marcy Sohn for your support and encouragement.

Solved

The Greatest Art Crime in History

Sneak Peek – Coming Soon!

Prologue

Boston – St. Patrick's Day, 1990

Two men dressed as police officers knocked on the side door of Boston's Isabella Stewart Gardner Museum. It was March 17th. St. Patrick's Day was winding down. It was 1:24 a.m. They said they were checking out a reported disturbance and needed to get inside to ensure everything was "*copacetic.*"

Upon entering, the criminals calmly announced, "Gentlemen, this is a robbery."

Within a few moments, the security guards were overpowered and gagged. And then duct-taped in the museum's basement, where they remained until morning.

Thus began the world's biggest art heist. $500 million in art treasure. Gone. And a mystery that would befuddle investigators for decades.

It took 81 minutes for the thieves to disable security cameras and remove precious works of art from their frames. They then made two separate trips to their car, filling the rear of their late model hatchback with the precious art. In the world of art theft, burglars are usually in and out in as little time as possible. But these guys were in no hurry. They operated as if they had all the time in the world.

The thieves snatched some of the museum's greatest treasures, including: *A Lady and Gentleman in Black*, by Rembrandt, Vermeer's *The Concert* (one of just 35 of the Dutch Master's paintings to survive today), and *Christ in the Storm on the Sea of Galilee*, the only known seascape painted by Rembrandt. They also picked up a self-portrait sketch by Rembrandt. Five sketches by French Impressionist Edgar Degas. A portrait of a man *Chez Tortoni* by Édouard Manet. And an ancient Chinese bronze vessel – the oldest item in the museum dating from 1,200 BC.

Strangely, they were also drawn to a bronze, eagle-shaped finial from the Napoleonic era. They added that to their loot while ignoring the museum's most expensive works, including: Titian's *The Rape of Europa, El Jaleo* by John Singer Sargent, the 17th century *Portrait of Thomas Howard* by Peter Paul Rubens and a 15th century priceless painting by Botticelli.

At the time of the theft, there were more than 290 paintings and 280 other pieces of art in the museum's collection, including tapestries, ceramics, furniture and documents. But there was no rhyme or reason to what the thieves chose to pinch. Authorities and art experts found their choices of what to steal odd. No single motive or pattern emerged. No one has been able to answer the perplexing question of why these specific works were taken...love, money, glory, barter, ransom or some combination of each? Nobody knew.

In the days that followed, descriptions of the robbery ran in newspapers worldwide. Sketches of the two perpetrators in stolen police uniforms wearing fake mustaches were widely circulated. But they looked like any thirty-something-year-old white guys in Boston. The FBI sent in its squad of art theft investigators, arguably the best in the world. In the early days after the heist, authorities had every reason to believe that the artwork would be recovered in short order.

World renowned artwork is extremely difficult to sell, even on the black market. The surest way to end up in prison is to try to unload a piece of art the world knows is stolen. Typically, thieves make contact within a few days and ransom back the art. The expense is usually paid by the insurance company, delighted to pay a small percentage of the art's value for the recovery. The new word for this is *artnapping*.

The Gardner Museum announced a $1 million reward for information leading to the recovery of the art. That reward would be increased several times in the years that followed. Hundreds of leads flooded the FBI tip line. Each required a time-consuming follow up. There were rumors of elusive billionaires, organized crime figures, slick cat burglars and sophisticated art thieves.

But none have panned out.

Chapter 1

South Windsor, CT.
The morning after the heist

The morning after the Gardner art heist, Vinnie San Giovanni walked into the Italian bakery he had owned and operated for the last twenty years. He used to love getting up long before dawn, starting his day baking with a couple of talented young bakers he referred to as *"fresh off the boat from the boot."*

By 7:00 a.m. his cases would be full of freshly baked cannoli, biscotti, cookies and other scrumptious delights. He'd then flip the switch to light up the neon sign announcing to the world that San Giovanni's Bakery was now OPEN.

He often wished that he could bottle the smell of his fresh coffee and baked goods. After all, they could bottle the new car smell. *So why not San Giovanni's Bakery*, he mused. Each morning there would generally be half dozen people waiting for the doors to open. His six tables turned over frequently. The stand-up coffee counter remained full through most of the day.

By the afternoon, half of the sweets in his imported glass bakery cases would be sold. At day's end he would pack up and deliver the unsold goods to the homeless shelter along with a large box to the police department and the fire station. Keeping the cops in sweets was cheap insurance here in the insurance capital of the world.

These days he starts work around 10:00 a.m. It's not that he's lost interest in baking or the bakery business, it is just that he has other interests. None of which are legal.

Vinnie's office is in the rear of the bakery. That's where the real money is made. The bakery is simply a front. His old man used to tell him, "*The best place to hide is in plain sight.*"

Along with a small crew, he keeps a low profile. He quietly runs his numbers operation, bookmaking, petty theft and loan sharking under the radar. He was smart enough to never get involved in selling drugs. Nor did he ever become large enough to call attention to himself. His cash is funneled through the bakery. And he pays his taxes. Well, most of them, anyway.

Vinnie never became a *made man,* mafia parlance for a member of one of the mob families. But over the years he has been quick to do special favors when asked by the bosses in Providence, Boston and Albany. He built himself a reputation as a smart man who kept his mouth shut. The bosses referred to him as a *stand-up guy,* someone loyal and trustworthy.

Everyone liked him. And so he was left alone to run his small crew, discreetly making a considerable amount of money.

Vinnie was a large man. Well over six feet. Tipping the scales at 300 pounds or more. Now in his fifties, he lived a quiet life. Cancer got his wife a few years earlier. He has a long-time *goomah* (mistress) tucked away in a condo in West Hartford. He visited her regularly. On occasion he took her to Mohegan Sun where they know him by name in the high roller's room.

Vinnie's daughter Angela just started her freshman year at the University of Florida. She says she hates Connecticut winters almost as much as she hates her father. She says that she is never coming home. Admittedly, Vinnie never was much of a father. But he had hopes that someday he'd walk Angela down the aisle and bake her a wedding cake his guests will talk about for years.

Italian gangsters often have nicknames. To no one's surprise, wise guys referred to him simply as, *The Baker.*

"Good morning, Rosie," Vinnie said to his long-time counter girl, as he entered the bakery.

"Hi boss. What are you having?"

"Bring me a sfogliatella and a cappuccino. With a couple of Sweet and Lows. I'm trying to lose a few pounds," he said as he unlocked the door to his office.

A few minutes later Rosie knocked on his office door with his order and a copy of the morning's Hartford Courant. Though Rosie had been with him for years and knew he had some *colorful friends*, she was unaware of his involvement in anything more than a petty crime here or there.

"Hey boss, you read about the art heist in Boston? These guys got away with hundreds of millions in stolen art!" she marveled as she placed his morning snack on his desk and left his office.

The newspaper headline shouted in enormous type usually relegated to a president resigning or a war ending. *"Millions in Art Stolen from Boston's Gardner Museum."*

As he read what details the authorities felt comfortable releasing to the public, he audibly mumbled a slew of Italian curse words. Vinnie knew that these heists generate a lot of heat on those who operate on the shady side of the law.

Later that morning, Carlo and Joey walked into Vinnie's office. They had both worked with Vinnie for over a dozen years. They were good earners and

Vinnie generously treated them to a more than fair share of their spoils. No one ever complained.

Carlo *Double Tap* Romano was Vinnie's distant cousin. Not many people took Carlo seriously because of his stutter. Few knew the nickname, Double Tap was not a result of his stammering but of the two bullets he put in the head of Mickey Ellis who made the fatal mistake of stealing from Vinnie. Joey *The Lip* Castabianca was a friend from the old neighborhood. They had each other's backs since junior high school. Joey had a rare condition characterized by the enlargement of his lower lip. Teasing Joey about his large lower lip often resulted in getting your face pounded by quick tempered Vinnie. Nevertheless his nickname *The Lip* stuck with him for life.

"Here's the dough I p-picked up from Dr. Melnick last night. Eight large plus the vig," said Carlo as he passed an inch thick envelope to Vinnie.

"Any problem with that?" Vinnie asked.

"No. I just showed him my hammer and he paid up right away. He is a horrible gambler. But that's good for our business. Ain't it boss?"

Vinnie shook his head and said, "He'd pick Yeshiva over Notre Dame given half a chance." All three laughed.

"Hey Vinnie, what do ya think about that Boston art heist last night?" asked Joey. "It is all over the news!"

"This is going to be a problem for all of us," Vinnie grumbled. "The Feds will use this as an excuse to bust everyone's balls."

He hoped his little operation was small enough to be ignored. Vinnie wanted them to recover the art and pay out a reward, more like ransom, and do it quickly. Since he had nothing to do with this stupid heist, he didn't care who got busted for it.

"What kind of idiot takes this much art? This is going to generate a lot of heat all over New England," Vinnie added. "Alright, listen up. We got some business to discuss. Joey, stop clowning around."

"What. I'm just sitting here, Vinnie. Ain't my fault I got a face that makes people laugh."

"It's your face, your voice, your whole existence, even your shadow's annoying," said Carlo.

Mocking being offended, Joey said "Oh, real nice, Carlo. This coming from a guy who once locked himself in a car he was trying to steal."

"First of all, that door had one of those fancy child locks. Second, I got it open, didn't I?" shot Carlo.

"Yeah, after I had to unlock it and get you out," Joey said laughing. "But I didn't mind. Watching you panic was worth it. You should've seen him, Vinnie.

Looked like a cat stuck in a fucking fishbowl," Joey snickered, shrugging as he exhaled smoke.

"Enough!" said Vinnie as he slapped the table. "I don't got time for your circus act. I'm dealing with comedians here when I need professionals."

Vinnie's glare silenced them quickly.

"Carlo, If you weren't my cousin's kid, you'd be the one fetching coffee, not drinking it, so let's get serious," Vinnie said, pointing his cigarette at them.

Leaning forward in a low voice Vinnie continued. "Alright, here's the deal. Tomorrow night, we hit the J&E warehouse over on Locust Street. Couple of crates need *relocating*. They'll be placed just inside the front door. And the alarm will be off. You know the drill—get in, get out, quick and easy."

"What's in the crates, Vinnie?" Carlo asked.

"Cellphones and some other small electronics. Stuff we can move fast. I gotta a guy in New Jersey who will take them. One, Two Three. Easy money," said Vinnie.

Chapter 2

Boston
The day after the Heist

The room stank of stale cigars, spilled whiskey, and bad decisions. A single overhead bulb flickered above the round wooden table, casting long, jittery shadows against the peeling wallpaper. Dante *The Bull* DeLuca sat at the head of the table, rolling a thick cigar between his fingers, his knuckles scarred from years of making examples out of men who thought they could cross him. Across from him sat Tony Marolo and George Lapardo, shifting uncomfortably in their seats, looking anywhere but at him.

He had already yelled. Already thrown a glass against the wall. But now, the room had settled into a dangerous quiet. Dante took a slow drag of his cigar, exhaled a cloud of smoke, then spoke, his voice low and steady, the kind of quiet that made men sweat.

"Let me get this straight," he said. "You two fuck-ing geniuses decided, on your own, without talking to me, to knock off the fucking Gardner Museum?"

George swallowed hard. Tony opened his mouth to speak, but Dante held up a thick, ringed finger. "No. No talking. Just sit there and let me process this." He paced to the side of the room, rubbing his temples like he was trying to stave off a migraine.

"You tied up the guards. Walked out with hundreds of millions in paintings. Not cash. Not jewelry. *Paintings.*" He turned back to them, eyes dark and unreadable. "And you *know* what you can't move? Fucking paintings!"

He slammed his fist on the table, making Tony flinch. George barely moved, his fingers gripping the edge of his chair like a man bracing for an earthquake.

"This ain't a fucking liquor store, Tony. This ain't some idiot in Revere runnin' numbers. This is the biggest art heist in history. You know what that means?"

He didn't wait for an answer. "It means every Fed in the country is going to be sniffing around *our* business. It means guys who never knew my name before are suddenly real fuckin' interested in who I talk to, what I own, and where I eat my goddamn pasta."

He took another slow puff of his cigar, then leaned in, his voice dropping to something just above a whisper.

"So I gotta ask myself something. And I want you to listen real close."

Tony and George held their breath.

"Are you two just *stupid,*" Dante murmured, "or are you God damn rats?"

Tony's head snapped up. "What? Boss, what the fuck!"

George sat bolt upright. "Dante, c'mon. You know us."

Dante flicked his cigar into the ashtray and gestured toward the darkened corner of the room.

From the shadows, Nicky *The Blade* Russo stepped forward. Thick shoulders. Cold, dead eyes. A six-inch hunting knife glinting under the weak light. Tony's breath hitched. George went pale.

Dante sighed and shook his head. "See, here's the thing, boys. I thought I knew you. I thought I had a crew that understood rules. But then you go and pull a job like this, behind my back." He nodded to Nicky. "And when guys forget the rules, sometimes they need a reminder."

Nicky moved fast. Before George could react, his arm was pinned to the table, palm-up. He thrashed, but Nicky's grip was iron.

"No, no, no!"

Dante raised a hand. "Quit the whining." He turned to Tony. "You know how many times I've had to do this? Too many. But you know what? It works. "

George gritted his teeth, his breathing ragged. "Dante, please!"

"You'll live," Dante said simply.

Then - slice.

The knife flashed. Blood spilled onto the table. George's scream filled the room. Tony lurched back in horror. George's pinky sat on the table. His other hand clutched his bleeding stump, his chest heaving.

Dante picked up his whiskey glass and swirled it. "Now," he said, voice smooth as silk, "that's your first warning."

George was shaking, eyes wide with pain. Tony sat frozen, his face ghost white. Dante took a sip of whiskey, then set the glass down with a quiet clink.

"You got three days," he continued, like they were discussing a business deal. "Fix this. Find a way to make it go away. Get rid of the paintings, send 'em back, I don't give a *fuck*—but if this ain't cleaned up..."

He nodded toward George's bloodied hand. "It won't be a finger next time."

Silence. Just the sound of George gasping through the pain.

Dante exhaled, like the matter was settled. "Now get the fuck outta my sight."

Tony practically dragged George out the door, the man's blood dripping onto the carpet.

As soon as they were gone, Dante leaned back, staring at the empty chair across from him.

Nicky stood nearby, silent as a tomb. After a moment, he spoke. "You think they'll fix it?"

Dante picked up his whiskey glass, took another slow sip, then set it down.

"I don't know," he said, his voice quiet.

He swirled the drink, watching the amber liquid move, then looked up at Nicky, his eyes dark as the ocean at midnight.

"But if they don't?"

He leaned forward, folding his hands.

"We bury them with the paintings."

And with that, he picked up his cigar and took another long, slow drag.

Ready to read more? Be sure to subscribe to be notified when SOLVED is released early in 2026

www.ericlitsky.com/contact-1

Also by Eric Litsky

Harry Would Be So Proud
Frying Pork Chops Naked
Pickles and Milhous Fly Again

Available in print, ebook and audiobook formats.

For more information and to be notified of new
releases,
visit www.ericlitsky.com

About the Author

Eric Litsky was born in the Bronx and raised in Queens in the middle of the post-war, baby boom years. He had a 10-year career in advertising public relations, followed by three decades as a commercial real estate broker.

Between his careers and raising a family, Litsky has been an amateur singer/songwriter, tango dancer, stage actor, and tuba player. *The Closing of The Day* is his first novella and his fourth book.

He resides with his wife, Norma, in Northern Connecticut.